ONCE THE SHORE

"Yoon's prose is spare and beautiful. He can describe the sea
more ways than seem possible without losing freshness, and his
characters' world is often quietly dazzling. . . . Yet the beauty
of these stories is precisely in their reserve: they are mild and
stark at the same time. By mild I do not mean cozy. Harshness is
always close at hand here, and no one is surprised by betrayals,
thefts, brutal mistakes of war. . . . Most of the collection's
characters move through events with a resignation or forbearance
rare in contemporary fiction. *Once the Shore* is the work of a large
and quiet talent."

—Joan Silber, *The New York Times Book Review*

"Yoon's collection of eight richly textured stories explore the
themes of family, lost love, silence, alienation, and the effects of the
Japanese occupation and the Korean War on the poor communities
of a small South Korean island. . . . Yoon's stories are introspective
and tender while also painting with bold strokes the details of the
lives of the invisible."

—Starred Review, *Publishers Weekly*

"Yoon, a New York City-born Korean American, writes with such
sparse precision as to create a visceral portrait of lost souls, each
searching in worlds both living and dead. . . . Yoon's writing
results in a fully formed, deftly executed debut. The lost lives,
while heartbreaking, prove illuminating in Yoon's made-up world,
so convincing and real. To read is truly to believe."

—Terry Hong, *San Francisco Chronicle*

"Though visions of violenc⸺⸺⸺⸺⸺ of
Once the Shore, Yoon is r⸺⸺⸺⸺⸺ss,

his stories are tender, lucent, and vital. . . . Yoon has described a perfect arc of time and geography, a whole water-bound world."

—Zoe Slutzky, *Los Angeles Times*

"*Once the Shore* heralds the arrival of a remarkable voice, a heartbreaking storyteller and chronicler of life in its infinite varieties. This reader is ready to proclaim *Once the Shore* not just the best debut of the year, but already one of its best books, period. . . . *Once the Shore* is short storytelling at its best."

—Tod Goldberg, *Las Vegas City Life*

Once the Shore

stories Paul Yoon

Sarabande  Books

LOUISVILLE, KENTUCKY

Managing Editor
Sarabande Books, Inc.
2234 Dundee Road, Suite 200
Louisville, KY 40205

Library of Congress Cataloging-in-Publication Data

Yoon, Paul.
    Once the shore : stories / by Paul Yoon. — 1st ed.
        p.   cm.
    ISBN 978-1-932511-70-3 (pbk. : alk. paper)
    1. Korea—Social life and customs—Fiction. I. Title.
    PS3625.O54O53 2009
    813'.6—dc22   2008019331

Cover and text design by Charles Casey Martin
Cover image © Brenda Chrystie/CORBIS

Manufactured in Canada
This book is printed on acid-free paper.

Sarabande Books is a nonprofit literary organization.

The Kentucky Arts Council, a state agency in the Commerce
Cabinet, provides operational support funding for Sarabande
Books with state tax dollars and federal funding from the National
Endowment for the Arts, which believes that a great nation
deserves great art.

This project is supported in part by an award from The National
Endowment for the Arts.

For my parents and my brother,
Chang Nam Yoon, Sung Jung Yoon, and Peter Yoon.

CONTENTS

ACKNOWLEDGMENTS

These stories first appeared, in different form, in the following publications:

"Once the Shore": *One Story*
"Among the Wreckage": *Glimmer Train*
"Faces to the Fire": *Salamander*
"So That They Do Not Hear Us": *Small Spiral Notebook*
"The Woodcarver's Daughter": *American Short Fiction*
"Look for Me in the Camphor Tree": *American Short Fiction*
"And We Will Be Here": *Ploughshares*
"The Hanging Lanterns of Ido": *TriQuarterly*

"Once the Shore" was reprinted in the *Best American Short Stories 2006.*

"And We Will Be Here" was reprinted in the *PEN/O.Henry Prize Stories 2009.*

ONCE THE SHORE

ONCE THE SHORE

ON THIS PARTICULAR EVENING the woman told the waiter about her husband's hair: parted always on his right and combed finely so that each strand shone like amber from the shower he took prior to meeting her for their evening walks. "There was a time," the woman said, "when he bathed for me and me alone." She knew his hair—its length, smell, and color—long before she knew the rest of him. Before he left for the Pacific. Before his return and their marriage and their years together. When she opened the door it was what she noticed first. And in the heat of the remaining sun, she swore you could see a curtain of mist rising from the peak of his thin head.

At this, she laughed quietly and almost at once grew silent and looked out toward the distant hills and the coast where, long after sunset, the East China Sea lay undulant, its surface of silver reflections folding over one another like the linking of fingers.

She was in her sixties, an American from upstate New York, who was a guest at the Chosun Resort on the southern side of Solla Island. She had arrived several days ago and no one was sure how long her visit would last. She spent hours on the back porch, dressed in loose linen outfits that hid the shape of her body. She insisted on tipping, ignoring the polite reminders that such a gesture was unnecessary in this country. In her possession was a single piece of luggage, the perfect size—the hotel staff joked—for a head.

Her own hair she let fall in the most graceful of ways, all the way down past her shoulders. It clung to the backs of chairs or the cushioned elevator walls or, as the maid noticed, it stubbornly refused to sink into the depths of the shower drain, clenched in a gray-white fist.

Her husband used to maintain navigation equipment on an aircraft carrier not too far from here, she mentioned. He was dead now, a few months having passed since his heart stopped just as he woke and attempted to flip the duvet away from his body.

On that morning she bathed him with a wet cloth. Lifted his limbs and wiped his brow. His comb she dipped into the water bowl beside her and then proceeded to brush his hair, gray now, parting it on the right as he had always done since the first day they met in front of her parents' home in a small town where, in winter, the snow was ceaseless.

. . .

The other waiters called him Jim. Short for Jiminy because a group of them watched the Disney animated classic *Pinocchio* one night in a conference room at the resort. The youngest of the waiters, they decided, resembled the cartoon cricket: thin limbs and a round head with big, wide, dark eyes. A smile as magnificent as a quarter-moon. And so they—all of them in their thirties, having worked here for much longer than the boy and used to teasing him—began saying the name out loud, calling him Jiminy, over and over again, seated in velvet plush chairs and rolling their tongues and smoking the hashish they had obtained from a Spanish backpacker in exchange for leftover food. They had difficulty pronouncing the name. The boy corrected them, using three distinct syllables. "Easier to say 'Jim,'" he told them, and they nodded with a drug-induced acquiescence.

He was twenty-six and originally from the mainland, seventy kilometers north, where his parents and brother still remained. After attending the university in Seoul, he went on to military duty.

It was during training exercises at sea that he first saw the coasts of the island. By boat he and the other soldiers his age circled it, marveling at the bright foliage and Tamra Mountain at its center, once a volcano, which rose nearly two thousand meters. Cars the size of pebbles moved along the highway, it seemed, without effort, without anywhere really to go. There, they were told by an officer, the distance from one destination to another never took longer than an hour by car, from the waterfalls, hiking trails, the caves, to the beaches and the mountain's peak. This fact stayed with him, long after his duty, long after he saw the island again through an airplane window as he arrived to look for work. And it was, a year later, what he told his diners.

His brother, a fisherman, often teased him about working at a resort. But he couldn't imagine working anywhere else. The snug white jacket they were required to wear like a second layer of skin. The sound of uncorking a bottle of wine in front of his tables. The warmth of dinner plates. Here he met guests from all parts of this world. And almost always the food was served outdoors on a long porch that faced two hills and the East China Sea. He was, every night, witness to the setting sun. And in all of these patterns he was assured of an ineffable logic that at once bound him to the resort property and at the same time provided him with a sense of openness and possibility.

Until last night, as he stood behind the seated American widow. Though it wasn't her, exactly. It wasn't the way the woman related the story of her husband's hair, to which he tried very hard to listen. Or the way the sun wavered on the crest of a hill, as though rather than going down it had decided to pitch and roll along the slope.

It wasn't any one of these things.

It was, in fact, the manager of the resort—a man who was very fond of Jim—who led him into his office in the middle of dinner and told him that his brother, while catching tuna, as he had been doing for the past few years for their uncle's company, was killed when a United States submarine divided the Pacific Ocean for a moment as it surfaced, causing a crater of cloudy water to bloom, the nose of this great creature gasping for air while its body collided against what could have easily been a buoy or some type of detritus.

But what keeled and snapped upon impact was a fishing boat. And within it a crew of fishermen. Their bodies, once broken, sunk into a dark depth, their limbs positioned, without effort, in the most graceful forms known to any dancer.

It was morning and she sat at her usual table closest to the stone ledge, occupied by the distant strokes of a swimmer in the outdoor pool. Beside her, at another table, a Canadian man was reading aloud portions of the news to his companion. The incident with the U.S. submarine caused the American widow to shift her attention. The bodies had not yet been recovered. An admiral gave a press conference and formally apologized for this tragedy, unable to give further information at this time.

Her husband used to clip articles out of the newspaper. Anything having to do with the Pacific. It was a type of hobby, she assumed, like collecting butterflies. He tucked them inside photo albums. He never showed them to her. She only knew about it because, cleaning out his study, she had opened one, thinking they contained pictures. Years' and years' worth of collecting. She immediately shut the books. It was as though she had opened her husband's diary and felt it wrong to do so, even if he was no longer present. "It just isn't right," she muttered to herself, returning the album to its spot on the shelf.

The waiter called Jim approached the diners with a tray of orange juice in highball glasses and when he placed two on the table with the Canadians, he lifted his hand very slowly, as though attempting to slow time. He furrowed his brows and rubbed his eyes and the widow stiffened her back as he passed and quickly took the order of another table without meeting their gaze. He had forgotten to slick his hair, she noticed, so it seemed dull under the morning sun.

She raised a hand. "Hello, Jim," she said. "I've been up since four. And I called room service because your dining room is never open so early. You should look into that, you know."

He tucked his empty tray under his arm and promised he would. She told him she had yet to see Tamra Mountain and he offered her suggestions on reliable drivers, who appeared at the entrance to the hotel every hour. To all of this she nodded vaguely, "Yes, yes," she added. "Tell me what else you know of this place."

Jim began to describe it as best as he could. If you were to think of the island in terms of circles, then the outer circle was mostly residential, including the cities and the resorts; farther inland were the farms and the forests, and at the center was the mountain that stood behind them. She had only glanced at it through the taxi window on her way here. And although it was always visible, she made no effort to take the time to observe it. She wasn't interested. Not in its presence or its impressive height or how most guests were determined to hike along its trails. For her, it was simply what identified the island. She had come to the right place. That was all.

"It takes no longer than one hour to get from here to anywhere," Jim said.

"Anywhere," she repeated, then smiled, although Jim didn't join in the merriment.

She concluded the boy was tired—that he had been up late and needed sleep. She could tell from the redness of his eyes, the way his shoulders slouched. There was a question she wanted to ask him but decided it could wait. Instead, she pointed her head as discreetly as possible toward the Canadians and said, "Terrible business. I suspect you won't look fondly on Americans after this."

The expression on his face was that of confusion.

"My husband. He was here, you know. Many years ago. Not here, exactly, but over there." She lifted a finger toward the coast. "Somewhere over there, I think. I'm not really sure, to be perfectly honest. But I can imagine it. And it would take exactly one hour. That's what I think, Jim. Like you said. Exactly one hour and we'd find it."

The boy asked whether he could get her anything else.

"Oh, I'm just fine," the woman said. "And you work too hard. Get some rest."

And here, before being conscious of it, she took his hand between hers and patted his knuckles. His skin was warm, his circulation excellent. She imagined the blood that flowed underneath these fingers, rivers of it, splitting like highway systems. How healthy he must be with such warm hands. He was a boy, she was certain, who didn't grow cold easily.

It wasn't hope he felt. That God was merciful. No, that was his parents, praying that their oldest son had found a piece of wood. Found the belly of a whale. He was, rather, unable to accept. There was a difference. Because for him, the event never happened. Not until the body was recovered. Until then, his brother was still fishing. On a boat in the Pacific casting nets the size of mountains.

The manager offered a leave of absence. His parents wanted him to fly back home. But Jim declined the offer. He continued to do his work. The staff was not yet aware of the circumstances. He made the manager promise. In this way, every day was like all the days. He wiped lint off his jacket. Tightened the knot of his black tie. Washed his hands before serving. His co-waiters called, "Hey Jim!" and he walked over to their tables to speak to the tourists about the scenic hiking trails and the best waterfall for swimming. There was much talk, of course, about the submarine incident over dinner, but it was conversation that wasn't directed in any way toward him. He lingered above them for a moment while pouring wine or refilling their water glasses and the more they talked, the more it seemed it had nothing to do with him at all. As though the event, once escaped from mouths, was no longer his, now fanned across the air in the realm of static.

When he could spare a moment, he often stood by the American widow because he had done so for what seemed like long before. Her shedding gray hair and linen outfits were a recurring fixture on the long porch where he, with a form of reverence, served plates of the country's finest cuisine. She was the one who stayed long after the other guests retired. Her fingers tapped the stem of a wine glass or the candle holder as she addressed the scenery in front of her—she always ate facing the sea—all the while knowing that Jim stood behind her right shoulder as the busboys cleared the tables and the rest of the waiters took their cigarette breaks.

And he listened. Listened to her describe a photograph of a young man—younger than Jim—in uniform with a stern expression and his hair cut short (how she mourned for his hair when they cut it), and the large fields through which they walked, passing silos and a stable where they once snuck in and tried to feed carrots to a stubborn pony, who, instead, bit her knuckle.

He remained behind her, listening, without knowing

exactly why. Perhaps it was her voice. The calm of it. The sudden laughter. Or her scent: the smell of lemongrass. Or because it felt, facing that distant coast, as if it weren't her voice at all but one that originated from the sea. He waited until she finished and only then did he respond by way of a brief comment or a simple nod and she would, as it grew to be her habit, take his hand between hers and tap his fingers.

"I have never been to your country," he confessed to her.

"You will if you want to," she answered. "I have no doubt."

He didn't tell her whether or not he wanted to; he wasn't sure himself. It seemed this place would suffice. Or maybe it wasn't an issue of sufficiency. Maybe going somewhere else was an act of remembrance, of where you were from. A world of mirrors in which you witnessed a countless number of things that could have occurred at home or anywhere. And maybe, just maybe, that in itself was worth doing now and again. Perhaps he already was. Like this woman who decided to come to this island of all places and now spent her days looking out at the water, at times with a finger pointed at a single spot on the horizon with the utmost certainty.

His brother used to take him out on a small motorboat their uncle owned. This was when they were all living by the eastern coast of the mainland, when Jim was eleven, his brother four years his senior. Their mother packed lunches for them, adamant in her rule that they should never stray far from shore. They were to raise their hands, palms facing land, and if the beach were hidden from their view, then they had gone too far.

They never followed this rule. His brother went where he pleased. And Jim trusted him with confidence, the way he hooked his arm over the rudder and leaned back as though he were reclining on a chaise longue. He smoked unfiltered cigarettes he had stolen from their father and the scent of it reminded Jim of damp wood. When they were far enough away his brother stripped to his underwear and shut his eyes, the midday sun on his chest, which was broad, a man's chest of which Jim was envious, as smooth and dark as the calm sea they floated over. He always took his clothes off on the boat rather than before they departed, as though he were only capable of doing so farther from the coast.

"We're going to find the middle of this ocean," his brother said.

They were pushing hard, perpendicular to the waves, and Jim sat near the bow, tightening his legs against the constant pressure of the water as it split beside the hull. He sat facing his brother, the shoreline receding behind the level of the older boy's shoulders. They sped onward. Twenty minutes perhaps. Maybe longer. And then all of a sudden his brother cut the engine and elbowed the rudder and Jim reached for the gunwale as they spun, fast, the boat rocking, and then slowing, slower, in their sight a single straight line that divided sky and sea, a line that traced their movements like the unraveling of a ball of string until, gradually, they were still.

Above them hung a quiet—save for water lapping against the hull, there existed no sound, not even of a bird or of a distant horn. And all around them lay the ocean, a great wide ring of it with just that thin line of the color gray with the boat its very center, and his brother then stood and raised a hand to his brows in the manner of a salute and said, "There. We've done it," and Jim followed his brother's gaze and where there was once the shore there was now water and where west once lay was now north, east, south, any one of them. How many rotations the boat had spun Jim couldn't recall.

The panic came in the form of an arc: slowly rising until the boy felt his chest clench and the joints of his legs loosen, and when his brother began to laugh in triumph, hopping and whooping, he knew then what it was to be afraid. It was the feeling of diminishment. And he didn't know what to do so he sat there gripping the sides of the boat as his brother, in his underwear, dove into the water and surfaced and shouted for him to come on down, he said, come on down, and Jim would not, shaking his head, his jaw set and his gaze fixed at that gray line. He heard his brother's breathing and then he saw, in his periphery, what resembled a fish jump up into the air and bite down on his wrist and all at once that line tilted and he felt the cold and the warmth and he shut his eyes and opened them to see that the sky was now a glowing haze of thick water.

This was when he screamed. Opened his mouth as the sea entered the passage of his throat and he heard the dull vibration of it against his ears and then he felt a rising, a lifting as water gave way to the heat of the sun, and all he saw then was a pair of thick, dark arms that enveloped his chest and he leaned back and listened to a soft laughter and felt a palm press against his soaked hair and heard the words, I was just playing, I was just playing, it's all right now, everything is fine. And then a hand appeared in front of him and within the thumb and index finger there was a compass, suspended just above the horizon.

"Here's our sun," the older boy said.

Jim reached up and took hold of it and, as the sound of the engine returned and they headed west, slowly this time, he fell asleep in the arms of his brother.

They reached shore at sundown.

"You're not going tell anyone?" his brother said, waking him. "Promise? You won't tell anyone?"

He remembered walking up the beach, his clothes still wet, and the look on his brother's face which, to his surprise, seemed so young then, so much younger than himself, his eyes as wide as a child's, his shoulders not so confident anymore, and he couldn't help but smile.

He promised. And then they held each other's hands for a moment, the way a shy couple would do, and by the time they returned home to their mother shouting about their where-abouts and ordering them to their room until their father came back to give them a proper punishment, the afternoon was already far in their memory, where it took the shape of not only a grinning secret, not only the conspiracy of two brothers, but of a campaign against the sea.

The Spaniard lived in a cave. That was the rumor she had heard from the boy Jim. For how long no one was certain. But lately he had been coming to the resort property to receive leftover food in exchange for God knows what. She saw him once, against the slope of a distant hill, with a walking stick, and she pointed at his figure and that was how the boy responded—that he lived in a cave. The American widow drew a mental picture of this man, outfitted in bearskin and smelling of lard, perhaps, or week-old fish. Hairy. She quickly dismissed this fantasy. It was, after all, the cave she was interested in.

"There are many," Jim said.

"I'm speaking of ones close to shore," the woman said.

"Many there as well."

It was evening, the candles lit. Her hand covered the folded newspaper on the table. A single body had been recovered, a man in his forties. The search continued.

She wondered if, among the missing, there were husbands. And she thought of the wives and whether they caught themselves in the late afternoons unable to remember what they had been doing or were going to do. She thought of the waiting. Of images of the sea that, years ago, dominated her dreams, all the more terrifying in its emptiness, vast and quiet and gray. Of how she prayed for her husband's safety, for his return, and how, in his absence, her love for him grew through memory, in constant repetition, images circling so that the effect was that time paused. And yet, time did not because a single day turned into another. She slept, woke. It was a feeling of both immobility and motion. This was waiting. She knew it well. And it was how the wives of the fishermen spent their days, she was certain, with the conviction that they were alone, regardless of the publicity, the news, the interviews, condolences.

A couple from Boston had shortened their stay on the island lest the incident provoke anti-American sentiment, which was developing on the mainland. A group of college students had formed a rally in front of the walls of a U.S. Army base outside of Seoul. There had been a skirmish at a bar involving a G.I. and a teenager. Jeeps had been vandalized with words painted on the windshields: *Go Home.*

But she would not. Now that Jim had mentioned the caves. Afterward, perhaps. Or maybe she would stay. It felt very possible to do so.

During a furlough, her husband and a friend joined a fishing crew and sailed to this island. They spent the day swimming and walking along the beach. In the distance their ship, a sentinel in the shape of a fingertip. There were no other reminders of what they would soon return to. Not even the distant roar of fighter jets. On that morning it was as if the war had paused for a day and while the fishermen rounded the island her husband collected coral and urchin shells, took photographs of the hills and the forests inland, and chased crabs.

There, on that coast, he found a cave. A wide mouth that drank shallow seawater at low tide, its walls as tall as the entrance to a fortress within the earth. He waded in. Not too far for it was dark. Far enough so that he could still see his own hands, sunlight concentrated into the shape of an egg behind him. He picked up a stone. And against the right wall, he inscribed his initials and hers and drew a heart around it.

There it would remain for the rest of their days, he told her. On an island at the opposite end of the world he knew was waiting after all this. Four letters and the shape of a heart etched in stone.

The first few times he told this story she believed him. And loved him for it, pressing her cheek down against his chest without speaking. They were in their thirties then and life seemed as they imagined, living in a town in upstate New York with enough fields to walk across in the evenings. Her letters to him during the war had gone unanswered. He had never received them, he said. But it didn't matter anymore. Because he had written against the wall of a cave. To her. Somehow, though she couldn't explain why, that was worth more than a lifetime of correspondences.

But when she asked him one day to see the photographs of the island, he hesitated. He lost the camera, he said. Stolen by a little Korean boy. And as the years progressed his story began to change. Not dramatically, but enough to make her pause, repeat the story in her mind. It wasn't a fishing boat. It was a small motorboat. Three friends instead of one. They were AWOL. It wasn't a stone but a shard of coral. And the more the story changed the more she wasn't sure herself what she heard on that first night.

He was getting older. Age transformed memory. That was what she told herself. And why say such a thing if it never happened? It was her inability to answer this that allowed her to forgive him. She wasn't angry. No. Just puzzled.

Later, she would find in a drawer a stack of photographs. Men beside a fighter jet spray-painted with the words: *Eat This MiG.* A group of young girls smiling shyly. Another girl bending over as her husband pointed a pistol at her rear. And one of the sea, flat and emerald, and set against the horizon a wide island with a mountain at its center.

She rushed outside to where he was changing a tire, her duster in one hand with feathers the colors of a rainbow, saying, "Is this it? Is this it?" until he snatched the photograph and told her to never go through his possessions again.

It was only in the evening, in bed, that he nodded, said, "Yes, yes, that was the island. That was it, baby. That was where I wrote to you." He pulled her shoulders to him and she felt a quickening and shut her eyes and imagined herself folding, refolding, growing smaller, and then she turned away from him, pretended to sleep, and felt as though she were sinking.

So when Jim answered that there were many caves she wasn't surprised. In any case, she told him her husband's story. About the initials.

"You would like to find them," he said.

In his voice lay a trace of skepticism. Or perhaps it was her own sentiment that she heard behind his words. Strips of the sea shone silver from the stars. A busboy blew out the votive candles around them.

"I would like to find him," she said.

Silence. She heard him sigh, shift his feet behind her.

She went on: "To wait. It is a fever. And I waited for him. But the man whom I knew, he never came. So I want to remember him. Not the one who returned. But the one who never left."

A breeze came in from the ocean and she watched the shadow of the candle flame swing across the tablecloth. It was late. She noticed the busboy lingering, waiting for her to leave.

"I would like to see a cave," she said. "Close to shore. A tall one. Before I leave. That's all."

It was then she managed to ask Jim the question that had been on her mind since her first day on the island. Why she waited so long—she had been here for almost two weeks now—she wasn't sure. Perhaps she didn't want to go at all, she thought. Perhaps the question was waiting for the right person.

And so she asked him and no one else. And he, after a short pause, leaned over so that his face hung beside her hair like a moon and quietly responded.

"I will take you," he said.

It wasn't a secret that Jim had grown an affinity toward the American widow. The Madame, the other waiters joked, a woman who, they were sure, came from royalty. No one in their right minds would spend more than two weeks at the Chosun Resort. Not with these prices.

"But someone who has nothing?" one waiter conjectured. "What does it matter to her?"

"What do you think, Jim?" another said. "Has she told you yet about her fortune?"

"Will you marry her, Jim?"

"All she'll do in bed is tell you about her husband!"

They had gathered outside the back entrance to the kitchen, on the dimly lit gravel lot where shipments of food were delivered every morning by way of a narrow dirt road that cut through a forest and around the resort property. Jim remained silent, smiling on occasion at their well-intentioned humor. For that was what it was. Their teasing wasn't out of spite. Perhaps a little envy. That was possible. Jim had found some other form of amusement in addition to watching movies late at night in the conference room or smoking hashish.

They also knew of his brother. Word had, of course, spread

among the staff. They offered to take his tables so that he could leave but Jim thanked them politely and refused, which at once confused them and brought upon a certain respect for the boy's dedication to his work. In short, they weren't at all sure how to proceed. In the end, they chose distance. They joked with him, as they always did, and never mentioned the news updates or their opinions on the matter—which ranged from rage to a shrug of a shoulder—although they saw him every morning in the bar watching television, skimming the reports in the paper, and speaking on a telephone to whom they presumed to be his mother.

And whether or not they knew it, Jim was grateful. Glad, he admitted, for the company and the harmless words and the patterns of these days, including the nightly gathering of the waiters, which always began at the back entrance of the kitchen.

They heard the footsteps first and then from the road a figure appeared with a walking stick. He was tall with short bright hair and wore shorts and hiking boots, his wool socks stretched up to his shins. He stopped a few feet away from them and leaned against his walking stick in the manner of one who had traveled from afar. From his pocket he handed over a small paper bag and Jim, who was carrying a plastic container filled with leftover food, walked over and asked if he could have a word.

"Gracias, Luis!" the waiters called.

The two stopped some distance away from the kitchen entrance, right where the road began.

"You know about the caves," Jim said. "Along the coast."

"Yes. Many of them."

"There's one that's very tall and wide," Jim said.

"Many," Luis said again.

"But you know the best?"

"The best?"

"Yes, the best. The biggest."

"The most magnificent," Luis said, extending his arms.

Jim nodded. He told the man that he had promised to show a woman a cave. "A family relation," Jim added. He hadn't planned on saying that but it came out naturally and so he repeated it. She was a friend of his mother's. An American. She wanted to see a cave by the sea.

Luis stood in contemplation. After some time, he agreed to meet them at a beach on the southeastern coast, and from there he would lead them to the cave.

"Sunrise," Luis said. "That will be best. Tomorrow."

With the container of food in his possession, he was about to walk away but then paused and tapped his fingers against his walking stick. He looked at Jim in a way that was indecipherable to the boy's eyes. He shook his container in front of him and said, "There is nothing more beautiful than eating with a full view of the sun at the very edge of this world. On the days I come here. To pick up this. That is what I miss."

And then he left and Jim watched him for some time, under the glow of a tall lamp, and wondered whether he really did live in a cave. And if he did, it was no different, he supposed, than living in a house. Perhaps his brother had found a cave, he thought, as Luis's figure faded. He could imagine it. With a front entrance that was always open.

"It is all set," the boy said when he called her room. They would leave before sunrise. She woke early anyway. At four o'clock. Starving long before the dining room opened. She had asked him up for tea. She would stay up a little later if he wanted to chat. "I have to prepare for our expedition," was how he replied, then told her she wouldn't have time to eat. Then he gave a short laugh and said good night. It was to be a surprise. How old his voice sounded on the telephone. "Good night," she said, perplexed.

And now she lay on a king-sized bed in the dark, unable to sleep. He was so kind, the boy. A kindness she imagined he had brought with him from infancy. She wondered about his family. His answers were always so nondescriptive. What she knew was that he was born in a place called Pusan and now his family lived in Seoul. He grew up on the coast. And siblings? She had forgotten to ask about that. She grew angry at herself for not asking such a simple question, but then the feeling subsided. There would be many more opportunities to speak with Jim. A lovely name. One that she always admired. James. For its strength. For its sensitivity.

Before sleeping, she thought of a great flat field. This was when her husband returned. They had yet to marry. In the dark they wandered, careful with their steps, for it had rained the day before. He led with a small flashlight and for every dry spot he placed his foot she imitated with such exactness that all they heard on that night was a single body in the midst of cicadas and the distant rumble of a truck on the freeway, its headlights filtered through the nearby forest, shredded and fading like frosted breath.

It was her blanket he carried. Light blue, pulled from her bed and folded and folded until it was a square, a pillow, a sack filled with a mysterious treasure, one that he revealed in the middle of that dark field. He dropped the flashlight and as it lit a fallen dome of white beside their feet, he lifted his arms and the cloth unfurled and hung for a brief instant in midair then fell like a parachute onto the grass. There, in the middle, lay their shape, their shadows already congregating. It resembled a tortoise. Their arms around each other. Their two heads meeting.

"There we are," he said, and pointed down at their silhouettes.

In that dark under a night spread with unknown constellations and the warmth that gathered at the very bottom of her stomach—there she made her promise. Because he had come home and this time wouldn't ever go away. Afterward, lying there, she twirled the beam of the flashlight across his pale body.

They had known each other since high school. Three lives they led. The first she would always think of as the evenings when he appeared at her house with his hair wet and groomed and they walked without touching, a good distance between them, discussing books or what they wanted to be. He always phrased it that way: what she wanted to be. The second was right after the war, when she thought of him as a swimming tortoise. And then that faded as the years passed and it was replaced by something she couldn't, to this day, articulate. It was the longest of the three. Though in retrospect, it didn't seem that way at all. In fact, the opposite: it was the first that lasted. For a good while. When his scent was of soap. When he would have done such an act as pick up a stone and write their initials in the mouth of a cave. Caged in the loose sketching of a heart.

They were to have a service for him. Without a body. A photograph instead. Jim received the call from his mother the day before. He would go; he had decided. His brother wouldn't forever be fishing, although he could always think of him in that way. Regardless of a service, a formality. It made no difference. He knew that now. So he would go. In two days he would fly to the mainland and return home. How long he would stay he was unsure. But there was one thing he was now sure of. He would stand there, in that room, beside the photograph of his brother, in front of a small group of the city's citizens, neighbors, family friends, anyone—he didn't care—and recount the story of finding the middle of the ocean. He would share that. And in doing so, he would regain his brother, pull him back down from the static of the sea and air. From the mouths of strangers.

And when the widow asked him, "Will you take me?" he said yes. He would do that as well.

He recruited two other waiters. Three was enough. They agreed in amusement, slapping him on his back and shaking their heads and describing it as the farewell party.

So at four in the morning they stole the keys of a resort truck and loaded it with the necessary products and, with the American widow, they sped away down the dirt road and through the forest and around the hills toward the southeastern coast. Their headlights spotted the foliage in a luminous lime color, the stars still clear and distinguishable against a paling sky. The woman remained silent throughout the journey, her hands against her lap, squished between Jim and another waiter. She was wearing one of her linen outfits, a light blue, with a white scarf draped over her arms. They all bumped shoulders whenever the truck skimmed over rocks.

It took less than an hour, as Jim predicted, and by the time they arrived at the beach, the sun was lifting above the horizon. Jim, with a hand on the woman's elbow, took her to an old log at the edge of the forest and told her to wait. From his pocket he took out a handkerchief and reached over toward the woman's head. When she hesitated, he assured her, "Just for a short time. I promise. A surprise."

The woman nodded, staring up at him. Behind him the sea was red and the sky thinned toward morning. She felt her heart. And the last thing she saw before her vision was covered in darkness was the boy's T-shirt with the image of a sailboat printed on his chest.

When her eyes were covered, he took her hand and squeezed once quickly and then ran to the truck where the three waiters carried the table and a chair down to the middle of the beach. They covered the table with a white cloth. Jim set down a plate, flanked by a napkin, forks, knives, and a teaspoon. He placed a saucer and a coffee cup to the left and two glasses on the right. The chair faced the sea. From the back of the truck they ignited Bunsen burners to heat the small silver trays that contained scrambled eggs, fried potatoes, and sausages. They opened the icebox to reveal a bottle of water, cream, pineapple, melons, and strawberries. The thermos of coffee was still warm. They changed into their outfits, black jackets instead of their usual white.

It was all set. They stood beside the truck barefoot. Jim began to roll up his pants. "One more thing," he said, and treaded down to shore. The waiters lingered by the truck, uncertain. The tide rose up to his shins. He looked back at the distant canopy of the forest, the flat peak of Tamra Mountain. It was possible, he considered, that this island lay at the center of the ocean, the place he and his brother never found. And thinking this, he began to cry, covering his mouth, rubbing his eyes with his knuckles. He waited for it to cease. He breathed, deeply, then slipped his hand into his breast-pocket and produced what resembled a harmonica against the light of the sun. It shone amber. Leaning forward, he dipped the object he was holding into the sea, like the beak of a bird, and then lifted it in a slow arc toward the length of his hair.

She had heard of fishermen in the ancient days, lost at sea, delirious and racing toward the horizon and the half-sphere of the sun in pursuit of illusions: some vision of land or of anything attributed to a country and its soil and the possibility of their feet touching a surface without sinking. She imagined that for the men who fell into the sea over a week ago now, perhaps one of them, if only for the briefest of moments, considered this as the water parted and the skin of what could very well have been a continent rose beneath them. That perhaps, before they keeled, there was this sense of a waking dream and, through it, a descending of peace akin to slipping into sleep. She hoped that it happened too quickly for them to feel otherwise—that by the time they knew this was the last of their days, they had already entered the sea and shut their eyes and given themselves to its depths.

This was what she thought of in the covered darkness of the handkerchief. And how, every night, she sent them a prayer. Not to a god but to their ghosts, whom she envisioned forever on a boat, riding the cusps of the Pacific, in search of images that existed only in the mind.

Like the one she saw at dawn as she smelled potatoes and heard footsteps and Jim uncovered her eyes, forcing her to squint, her vision blurred. There in the distance: penguins. Tall and slim, rising out of the ocean. Then they evolved into black-suited men walking up the beach, their clothes dry but their hair wet and combed and before them a table and a chair. She gasped, placing her hands on her chest. One of the men carried a thermos of coffee. Another a water bottle. Jim helped her to the chair and then leaned over to tell her about the menu. He then picked up her plate and carried it to the back of the truck and proceeded to arrange her requested breakfast. When he returned she picked up her fork but changed her mind and took his hand and tapped him lightly before she began to eat, the sun warming her skin and the tide closing in on the table legs.

Later, Jim introduced the American widow to a man who had appeared beside the truck, picking at the leftovers. They shook hands. With a nod Luis led them around the coast to a cave by the shore. He gestured to it with his walking stick, his arms spread, indicating that it was, in his opinion, the best. Then he bowed and said that he would wait for them on the beach, with the others. "Careful," he told them. And they were.

Jim held her by her elbow as they waded in through its tall

entrance, the ends of the woman's skirt forming a circle in the water. Their voices echoed the farther they entered.

There was a myth, he told her, that the island contained a network of underground passageways, used as meeting points for those who were persecuted for their religious and political beliefs. In the middle of the night, by candlelight, they would travel from all parts of the island and speed through the tunnels to a room somewhere. It was there they discussed the future of the island and its people, writing speeches and preparing pamphlets for distribution. No one knew where the room was located. But perhaps this was one of the passageways, he said.

They hadn't gone far. To each other they were still visible. They could hear the approach of the ocean. And Jim, his hair dry now, presented his hand to the woman. In his palm lay a small flat stone that she reached for and rubbed with the tips of her old fingers. He stepped away, stood behind her. Water cool and dark around his toes. He watched her. Her thin shoulders. Her shedding gray hair. The hem of her skirt afloat and her arm rising. With that stone she speared the wall of the cave and began what could have been a sketching, calligraphy, some form of design—Jim was not yet sure—or the words of a language long forgotten.

AMONG THE WRECKAGE

EARLY ONE MORNING IN THE SPRING of 1947, a dark blue trawler, once used for fishing, moved slowly across the flat of the Pacific. It had been abandoned by the Japanese on the banks of a river in Solla Island, and the old farmer named Bey had claimed it as his own. He now stood at the helm, above the deck. He was shirtless, his skin dark and speckled with moles. His pale beard hung past his neck, cinched at the bottom with a piece of twine. Below him, his wife, Soni, lay near the bow. She was asleep. Her right arm covered her eyes to shield the sun. Her hair, like a thin cloud, curved over her shoulder and across her chest. The sea was calm. Above them, in the shape of teardrops, flew albatross. The birds headed east, toward Japan. Bey was following them.

Two days had passed since they heard thunder and the trees shook as a cluster of long-winged planes stormed over their village. When they rushed to the coast they saw what resembled a vaporous tsunami rise up in the east, whitening the midday sky. And then the waves sped away, followed by a long echoing shudder. They recalled the bombs of two years before and remained silent. The noise faded. The waves calmed, the air stilled. Their world returned to as it was before.

They did not learn of what happened until the following morning, when the salt peddler arrived from the mainland.

The Americans, they were told, had been testing. This had become common. They targeted uninhabited islands. It had been this way since the end of the Japanese occupation. What the pilots were unaware of, however, was that the coasts of this particular island, east of Solla, were used by fishermen to collect seaweed and shellfish. And so the belly of these planes opened, releasing over seventy red-fisted bombs, and out of the hundred men who were missing was Karo, Bey and Soni's forty-year-old son.

They waited a full day for his return. And when he didn't come they set out to find him.

This was at dawn. Now they had been at sea for an hour. Already they felt the heat of the sun. Soni, for the first time in two days, slept. Though as soon as she was settled into it, the engine of a plane woke her. She rose, startled, her hair slipping off her chest. Bey descended the helm, gripping the rails. "It's nothing," he assured her, as the engine noise faded. He wasn't certain; it was something to say. He listened to their breathing and they kept in rhythm with each other. In the sky contrails were dissipating.

She believed him. He could tell by the way her face calmed, as though she were returning to sleep. She yawned and the sun hit what remained of her teeth. But then something caught her attention and she stood and pointed down at the waters. "Look," she said.

Bey attempted to follow the path of Soni's finger. He searched the vague shadows, the empty distance. She leaned closer to him. Her hair had become brittle, her eyes dim, her back arced like the blade of a scythe from her years in the fields. He used to cup his hand under her soft chin and bring her to him.

"Over there," she said, her voice gone quiet. "Do you see them?"

"What is it?"

"Dolphins," she said. "Look. They're leaving."

She was so certain. She kept pointing. Bey scanned the surface of the sea. Nothing. And so he shut his eyes and recalled their image, silver-backed and quick as spirits. He thought of his son and could not remember when he had last embraced him. He saw the boy in a field. He saw him wrapped in sails, running. He turned away from his wife, who did not know his thoughts, and he said, "Yes, they are leaving."

Bey and Soni had known each other as children. In those early years, as their parents spent the days in the fields, they would do their chores together. The houses there were raised on stilts and the ground beneath was used as a pen for pigs. They fed off the family's waste which Bey and Soni threw down through a hole in the kitchen. They washed clothes and bathed in the river, scraping each other's back with rough cotton rags, their bodies bent and shivering from the dawn water. They braided each other's hair. They wove wide-brimmed hats and moccasins out of straw. Every year, when the Japanese inspectors visited, they filled sacks of barley as offering for the Emperor.

Bey was thirteen when he asked the officials whether they took the grains for themselves. He was struck on the side of his face with the butt of a rifle. They were standing in front of Bey's house. He fell and Soni kneeled to cover his head, and when she looked up at the men they hit her mouth. When Bey regained consciousness, he saw her lying there, beside him, covering her face. What resembled the juices of berries leaked out between her fingers.

She lost her front teeth. They found one on the ground. The other, she told Bey, she had swallowed. Like a seed, she said. It was growing already. She opened her mouth for him to pour drops of water down her throat.

When he first kissed her he slipped his tongue into that space where her teeth had been. She pressed her other teeth together and surrounded his tongue. In this way he filled a space.

Their marriage took place when Bey turned sixteen. It was dusk and the winds from the sea cut through the trees and blew against the bonfire. They celebrated through the night and at sunrise the newlyweds went on a treasure hunt in the forest. The wedding presents—candies wrapped in wax paper, chopsticks, bean curd, pouches filled with small cakes—had been hidden throughout the village by the women and children.

Bey and Soni looked inside trees, on branches, under rocks, and moss. They searched without bothering to change out of their wedding clothes. Soni wore a silk gown with a ballooned skirt and wide sleeves, the top folding over her breasts and tied around her waist by a ribbon. Bey was dressed in clean linen pants that fell to his shins and a new pair of straw moccasins that Soni had made him. They stopped several times to face each other. In the early morning, sleepy and drunk with wine, they rested under a tree and she braided his hair and twisted it into a bun above his head the way all the married men did. They fell asleep there with their pockets stuffed with gifts.

With the treasure hunt, the amount of presents you were unable to find was the amount of children the wife would bear, the undiscovered gifts returning through a life. They found all but one. What that lost gift was no one ever identified.

Soni gave birth to their son a year later, on the floor of their house. Bey, along with his father, remained outside, facing the forest. They heard her and the frightened pigs brushing up against the pen. And then they heard the child. The infant was given to Bey to hold. He brought him close to his face. From his skin rose the copper smell of Soni's insides. Bey licked his thumb and wiped away the stains across the infant's head. He had his mother's nose, his father's thick eyebrows.

During the monsoon season, when the thatch of the roof whistled from the leaking winds and the floors shook, Karo learned to walk across the house, with care, as an old man would. First he touched Soni, who was attempting to boil rice, and then he returned and touched Bey on the top of his head. Back and forth he went like this. After the winds calmed and the house settled the child ventured to the window and looked outside in awe, as if they were somewhere else.

In the winters Bey carried him on his back to watch the sea at dusk. When it darkened they witnessed the constellations appear, one by one, and the child held on to his father's ears and leaned back as far as he could, swinging his braided hair. His breath puffed above them. He asked his father what kind of fish swam among the stars.

They were happiest then.

Karo grew to love the sea. And distances. When he was old enough, he joined a fishing crew. Soni wanted him to stay. To help with the fields. He would be at sea for weeks, months. Bey wished the same though he did not voice his concerns.

He left at the age of fifteen on a ship with mud-colored sails. Bey and Soni stood on the riverbank to watch him depart. Their son waved until the ship disappeared around a bend. They stayed there, standing, long after the ship's wake faded and the lanterns began to glow through the trees.

From that moment on, they would see him when time allowed it. And all the days that had gone so quickly, slowed and lengthened. Both Bey and Soni's parents passed away. It was the two of them now; and in each other's company grew the overwhelming reminder of absence.

Bey began to remain in the fields long after sunset, unwilling to return home. On some evenings Soni ate alone. While she slept, he took walks through the forest. Beside the river he imagined the limbs of trees as the masts of ships. He smelled the night water, light and cool. As the years progressed he walked farther. To the coast. There he undressed and swam into the sea, to the spot where the moon lay reflected.

Afloat, he recalled the treasure hunt and the single gift they had not discovered. He wondered what it was and where it now lay. He wondered whether an animal had taken the gift for its own purposes or whether it was still there, buried, or high up in a tree.

There were now days when it seemed that all his life he had been looking. As though he could not account for all the years gone, as though he could not yet claim those years as his own.

In the Pacific, a war had begun. And his son lived within it.

And Bey bathed in the luminous dark of the coast, scrubbing his back and soaking his hair and his beard. He stood upright to clean his chest. In his sadness he opened his mouth up toward the metallic stars and waited for one to fall.

.   .   .

The trawler lacked navigation equipment so he used a compass and a map Karo had given him on his fiftieth birthday. He had never seen a map so intricate before. The ones he had grown accustomed to were approximations, errors corrected over them again and again, revised by fishermen, a palimpsest created on rice paper, the islands unnamed. The one he held now had been drawn by a Dutch mapmaker, bought at a port on the mainland. It was well-proportioned and colored, the outlines of all the Pacific islands in bright green, each one named, though that mattered less. Unable to read, he guessed at their identities through their shapes. Here was Solla, one of the largest. And north, there, a portion of the mainland. In the east lay Japan; it was how he imagined the crescent moon might appear if one were to ever see it up close: flawed and ravaged.

Bey folded the map and stood beside the starboard rails, watching the sun distance itself from its reflection against the waves. The albatross hovered above him. The boat's low hum reverberated against the soles of his bare feet. He slipped his fingers through his beard as if sifting through sand. To his left, on deck, his wife sat and braided her hair.

He went into the cabin to retrieve a tin box and then filled a cup with cold barley tea from a bucket. The boat rocked against a wave and he steadied himself against the wall, discolored from the humidity. He returned outside and Soni took the cup with both her hands, bowing her head to thank him. He sat beside her and opened the lid of the box.

Inside there were dried squid, flattened, in the shape of spears, stacked on top of each other and the color of dust. Bey lifted one out of the tin and tore it in half, giving one side to Soni. They pulled off the tentacles, one by one, and ate in silence. It tasted sweet at first, then bitter, its texture elastic.

The winds were heavy and smelled of salt. He watched as she dipped her fingers into the tea and then pressed them against her chapped lips. In this gesture he saw how she had aged, as if she were shrinking each and every day. He was, too—perhaps they would be whittled to the size of a pocket. He thought of death in this way. A diminishing.

After some time, she said, "Do you think there are many?"

Twenty boats, the salt peddler had said. Moored along the coasts. How many men were on them was hard to tell. The hulls and the masts split, consumed by a deafening fire, and he imagined the men flung up to the clouds, as though a sea creature had spit them out.

She said it again: "Do you think there are many?"

As many as our village, he wanted to say, but did not. He told her he was uncertain and she accepted it, taking comfort in his statement, for uncertainty was what pulled them toward an island they had never seen before.

"He could have been inland," she said, more to herself as she continued to look out at the sea. There wasn't another boat in sight or the sound of a plane again, the roar, which was a sound that encompassed and paralyzed and forewarned. There was instead the blue of peace, the logic of seabirds.

It was possible. He could have been inland. Bey thought it as well. Who would not? Karo was prone to wandering. He liked to dock and see the town where he and his fellow crewmembers delivered fish. He brought back stories and souvenirs for his parents: some fruit, simply because it had grown elsewhere; woven bracelets for his mother, one she wore now, made from a strip of tanned leather; for Bey, a bamboo cane that he hung up on a hook, refusing to use it.

They began to call him sailor and waited for him along the river when he returned. "Sailor, what land have you seen?" they joked with him as he disembarked from his boat. "What gifts do you bring?" And he would say, "I have come from the stars, Mother, I have seen the planets." He bowed and they embraced him, his hair smelling of foreign coasts and Bey touched his son's face and pulled on the young man's beard, thick and dark.

He had grown taller than both of them. There was about him a calm, as though he took with him the flat surface of the sea in late afternoon and wore it like a coat.

Sitting beside Soni, Bey inhaled the air, breathing deeply. They would arrive soon, he kept telling himself. But stillness turned into immobility. It seemed the boat had stopped altogether, with equal parts of the ocean in all directions. He stood and walked up to the helm. No, they were moving,

albeit slowly, and they were on course. He listened to the
boat's engine. They were traveling as fast as it could go. He
descended again. He thought of his son's calm and hoped it
had remained with him until the very end. He kicked the floor
of the deck. Soni didn't turn; or perhaps she did. It did not
seem to matter.

The cabin windows were stained with dirt. Bey wrapped
an old shirt of his around a stick and then plunged it into the
ocean. His muscles strained as he lifted the stick, the old shirt
darker and dripping. He wrung it. He worked methodically,
like someone who had dipped a shirt into the sea a thousand
times before. And then with the shirt he wiped the windows, all
of them, leaving streaked arcs. When he finished he squinted
at his reflection. He lifted his hands up close to his eyes, close
enough so that he could see the lines of his palms. He had
lately found himself doing this often, guessing the distance of
his hands to his face and wondering whether it was lessening.
There were times when he thought he was losing his vision.
He stared at his palms and saw the geography there, the rivers
and the roads and the paths. He stretched his fingers. Between
them he saw blue.

The night before he had spent hours attempting to recall
his son, to distinguish his face. It was vague to him, out of
focus. Bey lay on a worn blanket on the floor, which he halved
so that a part of it could cover his body. Soni lay beside him.
The room smelled of sesame oil. The window was open and he

heard the wind. He shut his eyes; opened them. The light of evening splayed through the window. He could not clarify. He could not recall the last thing they spoke of, some final words.

At first he did not want Soni to go with him. She persisted. He urged her not to come. She called him selfish, a coward. She stood in the corner of the kitchen, her eyes ablaze like some demon. She made a fist and hit her stomach, saying, "He is mine," and they fought because fighting did not require thought.

Afterward, she lay in the corner of the bedroom and pressed the side of her face against the wall and said, "Karo, I am listening to your heart. I am listening to the sea. And I am scared." Bey was across the room, looking up at the thatched roof that seemed to spread until he saw a vast network of hands extending. Karo's hands were thick and scarred and calloused from the nets, from the war, and they were always cold and always beautiful.

On the lip of the horizon a dark object in the shape of a thumbnail rose against the sky. Soni saw it first. She stood and leaned over the rails of the deck, as though she thought the boat could go faster by her doing so. She resembled an eager child in this position. "Hurry," she called to Bey, and although it was impossible for the boat to go any faster, it did seem that their speed was increasing. The island grew taller and wider until its shape began to morph, sharp angles appearing that could have been trees or the back of a mountain. But the longer Bey concentrated on the image he grew more certain that it wasn't their destination. Perhaps it was a surfacing whale, swimming toward them.

But no, it was not a whale. Less fluid, less mobile. The shape of it was now fixed. It moved while being still. It shone metallic under the sun, which was now directly above them. A drop of sweat caught in Bey's eyelashes and he blinked, wiping his forehead. When he looked up again he saw what it was and he felt a tightening and the beat of his heart and he grew afraid.

"Seek cover," he told his wife.

He took her by the shoulders. Gripping the rails, she walked with care against the urgency of his palms. "Bey," she said. "Don't hold so tight." They exchanged a brief smile and he relaxed his grip.

In the cabin, underneath a mat, lay a door leading down into a storage compartment below the floor, a small room he never used. He lifted open the door and a stale, humid scent enveloped them. He held her hand as she descended and only when she was fully lowered did he let go.

Daylight stopped at the edge of the entrance. Soni's face was shadowed and her eyes were bright, like the eyes of the hares in the island's mountains. "You stay until you hear me say your name," he told her. "Or you stay until you hear nothing. You wait for the engines to fade." He said all this as though he were speaking from afar.

"Bey," she said. "I will be fine." She lifted her hand and waved. He pushed the door and watched whatever light was down there close like a shell. She was still waving. He replaced the mat. He looked about the cabin once more. He checked the closet that held his son's spare fishing gear, which he had never used. With the cup he took some of the barley tea and poured it over the net and the pole.

The engine he heard was much louder than his trawler; it sounded as if a crowd were clapping, sharp and rapid. He stepped out onto the deck.

The patrol boat was American. He noticed the colors and the design of the small flag folding in the wind. The boat, still rumbling, slowed as it approached the trawler. A soldier sat astern on a chair. In front of him was a long barreled rifle on a stand which the soldier panned, back and forth, across the length of the trawler, until it settled on Bey. Another gun stood at the bow, manned by a boy, it seemed, the chair larger than the width of his shoulders and chest. Bey counted the visible men: six.

He cut the engine. He placed his hands on the rails, where they could be seen. The patrol boat turned so that its port side ran parallel to Bey's starboard. There were words painted white onto the side. The two boats were five, six meters within each other. He could see the men's faces now, their flushed skin, their thick forearms. One of the men, however, was a mainlander, young, perhaps in his thirties. Through a mega-

phone he spoke in their language, translating the Americans'
words.

They wanted to know where he resided. What his purpose
was in the seas. His destination. How long he expected to be
out here.

Bey ran his fingers through his beard. Where his bare
feet touched the deck seemed fragile, unstable, as though the
floor would soon collapse. He concentrated on Soni's silence,
willed it, and wondered whether her eyes were open or shut.
He looked down to see that he was on his toes, straining. He
answered them with brevity, attempting to mask his island's
dialect as much as he could.

He told them he lived in Udo. He was fishing. For leisure.

"And the boat?" the translator said, his voice hollow
through the speaker. "That's your boat?"

"Yes."

The man lowered the speaker and spoke to whom Bey
assumed was the captain. The others continued to aim their
guns at him.

The translator and two soldiers were going to board. The
boat floated closer and the three of them hiked their legs up
over the rails and stepped onto the trawler's deck. They wore
black boots, laced up. He had never seen boots before. And
the men: they were tall and their skin was peeling around the
bridge of their noses; their eyes appeared bored, although their
hands were alert, gripping their weapons.

The translator approached Bey. "There are smugglers," he said. "From the mainland to Solla. Do you know anything about this?"

Bey shook his head. He lived in Udo, he repeated, not Solla.

"Yes, you've said that."

The Americans searched the boat. They wanted to know where his fishing equipment was. In the cabin, he said, in the closet. He took a step forward but was pulled back by a hand. The translator's fingers were warm and he felt each finger against his skin. He hadn't started yet, he called to the men now searching the cabin. He hadn't caught anything. He heard the clinking of tin.

"You're heading east," the translator said. "Toward Japan."

"Not that far," Bey said. "Far enough for quiet."

He heard steps, a shifting. The rattle of their weapons clanging. He felt the breath of the mainlander behind him and judged the distance between his own body and the man's rifle. He thought: if he heard the groans of a door he would go for the gun. He concentrated on how he would move his arms and his hands. He would use his elbow on the man first. He did not think of the men with the weapons as large as swordfish. He thought of a single man and a single weapon and shut his eyes. He waited for the door. He thought he would never know whether their son had survived, and he bit his lip and tasted the blood and breathed through his nose and convinced himself that he was forty years younger, with the strength of a bull. He formed a question and repeated it in his mind: What are these things you drop from the sky?

No sound came; the door remained shut. The soldiers returned to the deck, carrying a small tin box, which reflected the sun. They opened it, revealing the remaining squid.

"They want to know whether they can have one," the translator said.

"Of course," Bey said.

"Protein," the translator said. "They're lacking."

The two soldiers lifted a squid and raised it like a flag so that the others on the boat could see. Then they climbed back over to their boat. The translator followed them, but with one leg over the rails, he paused to look at Bey. He seemed amused. He said, "Old man, you are far away from home."

And then, as fast as they had appeared on the horizon, the patrol boat departed, leaving a wake that caused Bey's trawler to tilt. He steadied himself against the outside of the cabin wall. They sped away and the guns swiveled and angled up toward the sky. In the distance, under the light of the sun, he watched them tear the flesh of the squid and open their mouths and taste. One of them shook his head and spat a tentacle overboard. What remained uneaten the men tossed as well, flinging their arms, and the limp pieces arced up into air and fell and then vanished.

. . .

Although it seemed like less, it had been two years since Bey and his son had walked to the river to repaint the boat. It was the end of the war and Karo had returned bearing gifts in the form of unopened paint canisters. He had found them in a trash receptacle on the docks of a port on an eastern island, where he had spent the majority of the years, imprisoned. He had refused to fight for Japan. In a cave they took their time, inserting splinters underneath his fingernails, letting him bleed.

When he was set free and the prison camp abandoned, he took the canisters of paint, unaware of the color it contained. Altogether they had six tins, each carrying about two liters of paint, and they placed them on a wheelbarrow and pushed them along the trail that led to the river.

The Americans had by then occupied the island although in their village their presence remained unfelt, save for the occasional MPs that passed through in their Jeeps. They kept their distance, however, and it was as though there were two villages within one, brushing against each other on occasion. There were reports of violence in the central areas of the island but here the villagers' lives remained unchanged.

It was morning. The day was fine and the winds were slow. The trawler lay up on the riverbank, the same as when they saw it last. They had waited weeks to make sure no one took it. Far from the ocean it looked ancient and awkward, its paint dull and faded, chipped in some places to reveal rust. It had been his son's idea to claim it. They would take trips. They would take his mother.

With a knife they pried open the tins, anxious and eager to see the mysterious color. They had agreed that whatever it was they would use it. White, Karo had guessed. Green, his father said. Like the leaves. They bet a jug of wine. They squatted and huddled over the tins.

What they saw was white, a pool of milk. Bey was not surprised. He reached for his son and patted his arm. He said, "Sailor, you were correct," and he loved him and saw how much he had physically changed: his thinness, his eyes deeper and heavier; his fingers, the nails discolored, some of them still re-growing.

Karo never spoke of it. "We've missed years," was all he said. "But no longer." And Bey accepted this, as he accepted the seasons.

His son rolled up his shirt sleeve and, with his hand formed in a fist, dipped his arm into the paint canister. The paint leaked out onto the grass, and it engulfed his forearm just below the elbow. Slowly, he rotated his arm. Soon, dark lines began to spiral within the milk white and the lines grew thicker and the white faded, folding, until the paint turned blue, dark, the color of winter. He then lifted his arm and the paint dripped down his skin and his knuckles like dozens of rivers falling into the sea.

The project took several days. Throughout it all Karo

painted with a blue arm. Sometimes he pressed his hand against the hull and from a distance Bey was unable to distinguish between the limb and the steel and his son said, "Father, I have lost a hand, I have lost an arm, I am slowly turning into this boat," and he laughed but Bey did not, although he smiled and let him know that he had heard. He watched daylight bend behind the trees and the current retreat and Karo fade. The following morning he was returning to the sea, to earn his living.

They did not see him again for six weeks. When he returned, he taught Bey the functions of the trawler and pointed to certain areas of the boat and named them as though they were countries. They could have stayed there all day and evening. It was what Bey wanted. But Karo grew restless. "Next time," he always said, patting his father's shoulder. "Next time." And Bey watched from the boat as his son headed to the village, where his mother was expecting him.

They were not often seen together, the three of them. He was either with his father by the river or with his mother in the village. During meals, Bey and Soni spoke to him and not to each other. Bey did not know what they spoke of when she was alone with him. Marriage, perhaps. His unwillingness. Whatever words they exchanged with Karo they each took and kept private.

For every visit he promised to take them out to sea, on the trawler, but he never did. He kept promising. His work in the fishing crews lasted longer, sometimes for entire seasons.

One evening, when Bey and Soni were alone, he wondered out loud when their son would return and she responded, "It is nice to hear your voice again."

He almost hit her for that. The thought occurred to him, of swinging his hand across her face, of his flesh against hers. He was unable to look at her, shocked and afraid. He heard her undo the braid of her hair.

He left her and sat on the steps of his house, facing the trees. In the mountains behind the village, the engine of a truck groaned. The pigs shifted in the pen. Moonlight settled over the barley fields. The sky was clear and vast and the stars were pulsing like beacons. He had lived here for all his years. It was a life. There was love he was capable of and love that was desired. His wife he had stopped knowing. His son, it seemed, was gone before he could know him. He wondered then where all the lost things in this world lay. And who, if anyone, ever found them.

They had been at sea for three hours when the first of the debris began to float by them. They were small pieces of wood, some of them trailed by shreds of fabric. Over the starboard rails Bey and Soni watched them bob and hit the hull before they were swallowed by a wave only to resurface and approach once more.

Bey had waited until the patrol boat was no longer visible in all directions before entering the cabin. He found Soni, however, already standing in the room. They faced each other, in silence, as the trawler swayed, brushing water.

"You told me to wait," she said. "Until I heard nothing. That's what I did. And then I opened the door."

"Like we had planned," he said.

She reached to touch his arm and they stayed that way for some time. She said, "It is good to hear your voice." She gripped his hand and he led her to the deck where she returned to sitting close to the bow, watching the albatross hover over them.

Before long the birds faded up beyond the clouds and the island appeared along the horizon, flat and dark. It seemed at first to remain in a fixed distance from them. Soon, though, as if they had somehow unlocked what held it, the land approached at a steady pace and they were able to distinguish the forest canopy. Rising above it, like great balloons, was smoke. Soon they smelled it, too, the scent of burning as the winds pushed against them. By Bey's guess, they were perhaps three kilometers away.

He gripped the rails and held his breath. It was far worse than his imagination had allowed. The sea, all at once, was speckled with debris. They surrounded the trawler, like cracked and splitting glaciers. He listened for his heart. He concentrated on its rhythm and told himself to slow.

Later, he would attempt to recall what it was exactly that caused his wife to jump overboard. He remembered she stepped onto the rails and he rushed to her. He held her arm, said, "Soni," and she looked at him with an expression that was unrecognizable, one he had never seen. It was hatred, he thought, and she swung at him and he felt her knuckles against the side of his face and he let go and she was no longer there.

What was it? He wasn't sure. It could have been the island growing larger, the sensation of rushing they both felt. It could have been the evidence of destruction around them: the pieces of wood, the amount increasing the closer they approached the coast, some as long as the trawler. It could have been the clothes, a shirt, a straw sandal. Or perhaps it was the limbs they saw, a severed leg bent at the knee, two arms with their hands clenched together, the muscles still straining. The sea shining copper.

And Soni now in it. He saw her for an instant. Her white shirt spread across the water's surface as she swam away from him. He heard her breathing and then cough and he shouted but she did not listen.

Dense clouds of smoke surrounded the trawler. The air grew thick and warm, the sun fading within it. Bey's vision dimmed. She was gone. He cut the engine. He called for her. He heard the colliding of floating debris. He called again: "Soni." He stood there waiting and it was as though the inside of his body were escaping. He saw the world as gray and vast and impenetrable and he clawed at his chest and looked for the color blue. He thought of painting and stars and distances and what lay buried and he envisioned them on a map, positioned as continents he would never visit.

The winds grew stronger. And the smoke, for a moment, dissipated. It revealed the island, its blackened trees. On the beach lay the remains of masts and keels like the spines of ancient creatures.

And below him there was his wife. She was kneeling atop a piece of wood the size of a door, its edges shredded. She grasped the trawler's ladder for balance. She was drenched, her clothes revealing a body loosened by age, all her years contained in the folds and the pigment of her skin, like the inside of a tree. She knelt there and the water licked her knees. In her eyes he saw clarity. She motioned for him.

Slowly, Bey descended the ladder. His toes touched the damp wood and he felt Soni's hand press against his back to guide him. When he was settled, she pushed away. The wood tilted and then gained control of their weight and the waves and they were soon adrift among the wreckage. They kneeled and paddled with their hands, and their fingers turned cold and numb. They worked in silence. They kept low and remained under the haze of smoke. When a body passed them, they reached for the man. Some they held by the feet, others by the arms, neck, or hair. Whatever was closest. They picked them as if for harvest. The tide took them out to sea. Their breathing grew heavy. And, with all their effort, they pulled the floating men closer and lifted their still faces out of the water.

FACES TO THE FIRE

SOJIN KNEW HIM ONCE though that was a different life and then he left and she grew older. Now he had returned. She heard that. This morning, from her neighbor. "Sojin," the woman said, pulling weeds from her front lawn. "Sojin, did you know? Kori is here." And the news, like a premonition, brought on the certainty that her days were about to change, alter from their accustomed rhythms, as though the entire island had tilted against the tides and shifted in its geography so that for a brief moment the landscape was unrecognizable. She smoothed a crease in her cotton skirt and then, as she did every day, walked along the road that led to the town.

At the store she waited for him, assuming he would come, although it was presumptuous to think he knew she worked in the town now. Perhaps he was at the house, with her father. Perhaps he was looking for her. Perhaps she would look for him. Her thoughts revolved, afloat, never landing. The hours went quickly. She sold a T-shirt, camera film, water, candy, postcards, a map of the hiking trails around Tamra Mountain and the nearby waterfalls.

She had done well for herself. She could say this much. She owned the shop, one of the largest on the western part of the island. This would be the fifth spring her store kept business. A good month remained before the monsoons came and the wet heat lingered along the slopes of the hills. Last winter she turned thirty. It had been fifteen years since Kori left on a seaplane flown by a postman. She remembered the engine noises, the water spraying, then the quiet and the plane ascending. He would have been eighteen then.

The early evening arrived. Because of her father she had recently begun to close the shop before dark. But today she stayed on the sidewalk a moment longer, leaning against the metal shutters she had pulled down over the storefront window. The sun disappeared behind the distant forest. The headlight of a moped swung past her. Two boys fed pigeons and then chased them, the birds fleeing to rooftops. An old woman led a tour across the street, lifting a red parasol into the air.

It was a different island now. Mainlanders came for weddings. Foreigners visited the beaches. In the town, streetlamps had been installed, brightening the houses and the signs of the new restaurants that remained open until the late hours. There was a store where visitors could rent snorkels and then board a bus to the coast. A hotel and country club had been built beside the town and on some nights, after her father was asleep, she sat on the fence to watch the golfers on the driving range, the arcs of their swings gleaming under floodlights. She did not know what he would think of all this. Whether it made a difference.

She herself lived on an unpaved road at the edge of town, across from a field where the cows grazed. The houses there were single-story and painted white. Hers stood at the end. By the time she returned it was dark and she glanced through the windows before heading inside. From her father's bedroom came the sound of a television. He was sitting on the couch she had moved in there. He wore a cardigan and his hands were clasped over his lap. In the past year a faint scent of staleness had appeared in his room. She was unable to get rid of it and no longer bothered to try.

"Papa," she said. "Did anyone visit today?" His face was lit blue from the screen and she thought she saw him shake his head. She looked about the house—nothing to suggest a visitor. Perhaps her neighbor had been mistaken, she considered, and then apologized to her father for her tardiness.

In the kitchen she cooked noodles, cracking eggs into the broth. She brought him to the table and tucked a napkin into his shirt collar. She told him about her day, as she always did. He sat hunched over the bowl, his cane hooked to the back of the chair. Thin lines of dried blood were on his cheeks from where he had cut himself shaving. His gray hair had grown past his ears and she reminded herself to trim it.

He had been in Seoul at the start of the war when the bridge was blown. In her bedroom there were photographs of him as a young man in uniform. Beside those were ones of herself as a child with her mother, one under the shade of a tree and another on the coast. The room was sparsely decorated; there wasn't much else. There was a hook where she hung her shop keys, which were tied to a string she wore around her neck throughout the day. On a bureau was her mother's jewelry box. After dinner, while undressing, she tried on the necklaces and the rings, the chains cold against her chest. They didn't look as lustrous on her as they did in the box, she thought. Gold, she assumed, but had never bothered to verify it.

The bathroom was in the old style, with the drain in the middle of the tiled floor. She filled a washbasin with cold water and used a plastic ladle to pour the water down her shoulders and back, scrubbing with soap and a cloth. She felt the day ending and shut her eyes and hummed folk songs. As a child she would wash herself by moonlight, with the window open, and watch her neighbors, the cows, the moths, the world passing. It seemed like something only a child would do, she thought, now that she was older, though sometimes she was tempted to do it again. Once, she looked up to find Kori there, by the window, and she had flung the bucket of water at him and he had run back into the forest, drenched and laughing.

She was washing her hair when she heard a tapping on the door. "One minute," she called.

"Are you in here?" her father said, pushing the door open with his cane.

Sojin rushed to her towel and covered herself. He wouldn't have noticed anyway, but all the same her shoulders tightened and her face flushed, she couldn't help it. Cold air followed him from the hall, the scent of their dinner. He placed both hands on the cane and leaned forward, forming words with his dry lips, though none came forth.

"What is it, Papa?"

"Someone came by for you today," he said.

"Yes, Papa," she said. "Who was it?"

His eyes were gentle, apologetic. "No, no, I am sorry," her father said. "They came by for Sojin. Not you, my dearest."

And then he shut the door behind him and she listened to the beat of his cane and his heavy feet as he returned to his room to watch television. She stood there clutching her towel. She heard the flicker of the streetlamps beginning to burn, the hollow sound of water draining. Quickly she dried her hair. There was still shampoo in it, spots she missed, though she wouldn't notice until later as she lay on her mattress, unable to sleep, sliding her fingers through its length and smelling chamomile.

Born without a father, Kori, as a boy, lived with his mother in a village in the forest, close to the hills. Where the other whores live, the neighbors said. Rumors spread. His mother had entertained American soldiers during the war. Still did, the students used to say, as if from experience. Kori neither denied nor confirmed the accusations. The mute, they called him. His mother, when she was seen on the street, wore short skirts and sunglasses like the Hollywood movie stars. Presents, it was assumed, from her customers.

He and Sojin attended the same elementary school. She spoke to him because he was alone. She was seven. He was two or three years older. It wasn't out of sympathy that she approached him. It was because in her shyness she was unsure of how to join the groups of boys and girls scattered about the playground every afternoon. So she picked the single boy and circled him, widely at first, then narrowing, while he kept a ball of tape in the air with his foot. His legs were thin and tan. And it was only when he missed and the ball thudded into the red dirt that she took a piece of sesame candy from her pocket to give as an offering. She watched him chew, his mouth revealing crooked teeth. She picked up the ball and attempted to keep it aloft. She failed and she looked at him and he did not laugh. He said, "Try again," and she did.

When he was older, boys began to approach him, other times men. They called him names. He fought them no matter how many there were. Sojin did as well. They used their fists, their nails, their feet. They compared bruises. Once there were six, older and drunk. He and Sojin were walking down the main street. He was twelve years old then. The men took him by his arms and legs and carried him to the center of the town. He thrashed. She saw his muscles strain, his wild eyes. She chased them and hit a man against the side of his head. He turned and slapped her and from the ground she watched them take Kori's pants off and beat him. They were quick. They picked him up and put him in a car.

Sojin ran to her parents but before she could speak her mother saw her dirtied clothes and the redness along the side of her face. "Was it Kori?" her mother kept on insisting. When Sojin didn't answer they sent her to bed. "Enough," her father said, and forbade her to ever see the boy again. In the middle of the night she snuck out of her house to search for him.

At dawn she found him asleep at the edge of the forest, the bruises on his thighs the color of persimmons. He opened his eyes. She lay beside him and they looked up at a clear sky and spoke of the sea.

From then on, ignoring her parents, Sojin left the house while they slept. Her nights became days. Kori bought a motorbike and they rode to the waterfalls and the caves. They dipped an old T-shirt in gasoline, wrapped it around a stick, and lit it. They moved through the narrow space of a cave, guided by the torch, following their shadows against the curving walls. They went in as far as they could, the cave enclosing them, and they waited for the torch to burn out and then they raised their voices and listened to their echoes and imagined they were in the belly of a whale. In the darkness they felt themselves slipping, as though they were being swallowed, growing smaller, moving backward through time.

He never talked about his mother. She never asked. Not once did she visit his house or meet the woman. She grew used to this. They lived in fantasy and that was another life and they were young.

It changed with the fire. An entire neighborhood, in a matter of hours, gone. No more whores, one of her neighbors said, more concerned about the trees. They never found the body of Kori's mother.

After that Sojin saw less of him. She spent afternoons in the grass, looking into the destroyed forest. Often she found herself pausing with her house chores, listening to footsteps approach the road. Sometimes, during the nights, she spotted him at the edge of the field and went to him. They met in the high grass and stood there together as if they were travelers who had recognized each other. They spoke politely. He did not stay long and she watched as he continued across the field to wherever he was headed.

Kori, eighteen years old, left the island that winter. He was going to find work on the mainland. He was going to be rich. She couldn't convince him otherwise. Then write to me, she said. He promised he would. He never did.

She used to dream of him walking across the peninsula like Johnny Appleseed. In the early months it was like this for some time—her imagination with him, across the strait and not where she was, her body moving without her, it seemed, without permission. A year turned into another, the seasons repeating. She turned twenty, then twenty-five. She opened the store. Her mother grew ill. She thought less of him and of the fire until it was only an occasional memory. She took care of her mother instead. She spent the evenings at home.

Her mother passed away while Sojin was at work. She was found lying on the rush mat that she had preferred over a mattress. Her ear was pressed against a portable radio. It had awoken her husband in the morning and before he left to gather eggs, he had told her to shut it off. When he returned it was still on, tuned to a station that played swing music. She died grinning. With saxophones and trumpets.

It wasn't until the late afternoon of the following day that she saw him. She had come to the store early and propped the door open, listening to the radio at a low volume—news about a port construction, a US Army base, a sailboat accident, a series of thefts in a northern village. A small group of teenagers browsed the aisles. A man dressed in a tuxedo drove down the main street in a golf cart, holding a megaphone and announcing discounts at the driving range, "Two buckets for the price of one!"

She was arranging pinwheels beside the counter when he appeared at the window, leaning forward to view the displays. She held her breath. She recognized his narrow shoulders and his arms, their slimness, like the necks of swans. She knew his walk, the way he moved carefully past the window and into the store, as if worried of intruding. He was taller than she remembered him being. He had aged, of course. The boyish skin had become taut, darker, his jawline more defined. His hair was longer, falling past his eyes, which were alert and bright. He rested his elbows against the counter. He smelled of the ocean.

"You're here," she said. "You've come."

He had arrived the day before last. Had he been back before? she wondered. The question seemed silly once she thought it and so she asked him instead whether he was just visiting. What she wanted to know was whether he had come to stay but she didn't say that either. She was shifting her weight from one leg to another, she realized, and stopped.

"I'll stay for a bit," Kori said, and smiled in that shy way of his while looking at the gifts she sold.

He motioned for her to follow him outside. The street was crowded, people stopping to read restaurant menus, a line forming for the bus to the coast. He pointed to the left, over the country club, far beyond Sojin's neighborhood. The man in the tuxedo drove by again, honking the horn and waving.

"Look higher," Kori said.

Scattered across the hills were a few shacks, efficiency homes, and a narrow road that wound around the slope. The houses there were fairly new, built fast and cheaply in the late sixties, after the fire, when housing was needed. She hadn't realized anyone still lived there.

"The one on the left," he said.

The sun was high and she lifted her hand and squinted. She saw what looked like two windows. Surrounding it were trees, in their thickness the semblance of invulnerability.

"It's mine," he said. "I bought it."

She congratulated him. Home was the start of things, she told him. He agreed, his eyes alighting on each passerby. They grew silent, standing there among the pedestrians. Voices hung in the air and she felt them against her skin, thick, like a curtain.

He asked about her father. Married to the television, she said, to make a joke of it. He was doing fine, she added. It seemed the sensible answer, although the truth was that he was dying and there wasn't much left in his body to be taken.

She invited him to dinner. "I don't cook as well as Mama," she said, wiping her forehead, damp from the afternoon heat.

"I am sorry, Sojin," he said. "I should've written. I would've come."

"It's all right," she said. "We thought of you."

They noticed a man waiting at the register inside.

"I'll see you," he said.

"I'll see you, Kori," she said, and took pleasure in saying his name, already feeling as though he had never left. It occurred to her, watching him move through the crowd, that time, in some ways, had nothing to do with how you thought of someone. And she did not know how that was possible because time was, she thought, how you defined yourself. It was what made you and what finished you as well.

The man in the store came outside and began to speak but she couldn't understand him. He wore sunglasses. He was tall and his dark hair was long and tied by a rubber band. She smiled at him, attempting to decipher the words in some way. He gestured with his hands. She didn't know what to say so she watched his fingers. They were like birds. She tried to guess his intentions. A restroom? A taxi? The ocean? Schoolchildren approached and she was forced to step closer to him. She, too, motioned with her hands. For a moment, it was as though she were looking through a mirror, both of them with their hands raised, forming shapes, and she wasn't sure why but she grew afraid and stopped.

She said, "I'm sorry, I can't help you," and returned inside. Eventually the man wandered away and she checked the counters to see if anything was missing. By then Kori had gone as well and the shop was empty. She searched for music on the radio. She felt a breeze; the pinwheels spun. At the window there were faces pressed against the glass, looking in.

He was their first guest in over a year. They sat at the kitchen table, her father at the head. A large red cloth had been placed over the table, covering its metal legs and its plastic top stained with oil. Her father ate the rice noodles slowly, lowering his mouth to meet his chopsticks. They were quiet at first, listening to the cars on the road and a child's laughter. Through the window behind Kori was a view of the darkening field and the surrounding woods.

He had worked at the railway, he told them, as a conductor. He wore a uniform and a cardboard hat and punched holes into tickets. He straightened his shoulders and said, "Tickets, please," in a stern voice and Sojin laughed. He saw the country in this way. From Pusan to Seoul, and up and down the coast. There was decent money to be earned, especially on the longer trips, but the time had come to leave it.

"This is about as good a home as I can imagine," he said. He had begun thinking about that these past years, now that he had been gone for so long. It was why he returned. He found little comfort elsewhere. There was childhood here, the memory of his mother. Her death left him with an emptiness, he said, and spoke the words calmly. Sojin didn't answer. Perhaps all his life he had been striving to fill it, he added, and had looked everywhere but the very place where it started.

"She was a good woman," he said.

"We were too hard," Sojin said, although she meant others and not herself. "It was a different time."

"Do you think so?"

She couldn't tell if he meant it earnestly or with sarcasm. "Yes," she said, conscious of her sincerity.

After dinner her father retired early to his room and she

showed Kori around the house. In the hallway he studied the watercolors and the framed medal her father had earned for helping civilians cross the Han River during the first days of the war. On a shelf he examined the wooden animals she had purchased at a flea market. He walked through the rooms as though he were at a museum. In Sojin's bedroom he commented on each photograph, then he looked around at the vase on her desk, a notebook, and the shop keys hanging on the wall.

"I thought you'd be married," he said. "I thought there would be children."

She laughed. "I forgot," she said.

He pointed at the plain wooden box on the bureau. She opened it and showed him the necklaces and the rings. "It's what I kept," she said. "Of hers."

"You never wear them," he said.

"No."

"You should." He lifted one of the necklaces to the light, admiring the chain and the pendant in the shape of a teardrop. "And you're well?" he asked, meaning the business.

"We have tourists now," she said. "You saw. It's more than I could ever want."

He seemed pleased but distracted. He returned the necklace to the box. "It'll hold you, then?" he asked, and she nodded.

He was let go, she realized suddenly. It was why he returned. With his savings he bought a home up in the hills, one he could afford. He didn't want to tell her. She felt affection for him then and wanted to reach for his arm but chose not to.

"And you'll work here?" she said.

"At the club," he said. "In a little while. Cutting grass, keeping the course trimmed. I'll work the machines."

"You'll do well."

On the back steps they drank tea, looking out at the hills and the last light of day. The fields were quiet, the air cool. In the dark, televisions flickered behind half-shut curtains.

"You must show me the house," she said.

"Soon," he said.

She offered help if he needed it, unpacking boxes, cleaning.

"I can manage," he said.

She was surprised at her disappointment. And then she remembered. "I have something for you," she said, standing. "Something I've been waiting to give you."

She led him around to a shed. She opened the door and went inside to turn on the light. She waved away the floating dust. Mosquitoes and moths gathered around the bulb. Her bicycle stood against the far wall, along with a wheelbarrow and tools. Beside that was something covered in a tarp. She lifted the tarp to reveal a blue motorbike leaning on its stand.

"Bring it home with you," she said.

"You saved it," he said, astonished.

"Well, of course I did."

She drove it on occasion to the coast but she didn't tell him this. She handed him a plastic jug containing fuel. He looked doubtful as he pushed the motorbike out of the shed, filled the tank, and wiped the seat with his hand. He started it. It rumbled, then hummed. He switched on the headlight and a slim white path spread against the grass and the trees. A neighbor looked out his window but then lost interest. In the field a brother and sister were kicking a ball.

He asked if she wanted to go for a ride but she shook her head. "Not tonight," she said, mentioning her father.

From the front of her house Sojin watched as Kori headed down the street. She finished her tea and drank his as well. She stayed to see the glow of his headlight move up the hills to his new home, expecting it would. Instead it cut through the road in the woods and then dimmed. She held the cups, unsure of where he had gone.

He used to spend his nights in the burned forest. She followed him once, from a distance, guided by his flashlight. He carried a small rucksack. He stopped often and bent down on one knee, speaking to himself. Remnants of the fire lay scattered everywhere. He collected pots and knives, mirrors and melted lipstick canisters. He found watches and rings and necklaces and wore them. He unearthed a possum's skull and called it human.

Throughout that week he visited the store every day. "Getting the house ready," he told her. At the start of the weekend Sojin prepared lunch and dinner for her father and then she and Kori drove along the coastal road on his motorbike. She held him by his narrow hips. To their left lay the ocean, the tide high in the late afternoon. There were surfers, three of them, wearing wetsuits the color of sealskin, their bellies against the boards, each wave lifting them. To the right was the forest and beyond that the peak of Tamra Mountain at the center of the island.

They went to the caves. She hoped, like a child, that they would use a shirt and a stick for a torch. "Did you bring them with you?" she joked with him, taking his arm. They sat inside the cave and listened to the hollow sound of water dripping and she thought of whales. She shut her eyes. She felt the walls move, the way she used to imagine, and the world receded with the light of day.

The next week, in the evening, they went to the beach. Campers were there now and she heard the various languages spoken among them. Some lit a bonfire. Sojin and Kori sat against a hollowed log at the edge of the woods. Smoke towered up toward the stars, obscuring the sky, turning it violet. She was content to observe the large crowd and thought now that time had everything to do with how you thought of someone and that it had helped him and she was thankful. She planted her palms against the sand, wondering how long the beach had existed, how long it had felt the sun and been cooled by the stars. The sand formed to the shape of her body and she found comfort in this.

She smelled the sweetness of the ocean, heard the slow hum of the swells. Down the beach, the drunks poured vodka into the flames and then danced. A girl, tall with blond hair woven into thin braids, stood to stretch. Sojin saw a man who resembled the one who had come to her store, the one she couldn't understand. He sat beside a woman and their mouths moved. There were others, too, their faces familiar against the fire.

"It's the settled life I want," Kori said. "You yearn for that after being away."

She believed him because he knew it better than she did. She supposed staying here was what she had always wanted, that by not leaving, she had made a choice. Or perhaps there had never been a choice and that the town, this island, had kept her. She had been willing. Still was.

He went to retrieve his rucksack from the motorbike. It was small and dark blue, made of nylon with heavy zippers. He took out a notebook, one he used when they were children, he said. She hadn't known. He opened it now to show her what he had written—*I have found three types of trees in the hills, her eyes change color*—statements that made little sense to him anymore. But he wanted her to see it, he insisted.

It wasn't charity, she said to herself, looking at him. It wasn't that. It wasn't sympathy either. There was a life in this and she felt both the old hope and the questions, her lack of courage. There was affection still but at this moment she wasn't sure whether she had ever known him or had known him too well.

There was loneliness here, it rose from her skin like a scent, she wouldn't deny it. There were the men who were drawn to that. She remained silent, bringing her knees up toward her chest. He took her hand.

She thought of the days when she did not see him and the days when she looked for him. She thought of how they used to fight the boys and kick balls of tape and it all seemed to her just then that it wasn't her at all but a different person, one that had left. The caves, too, even though they had visited them a week ago. The memory was already slipping. And she did not know why.

She was surprised at the words she spoke: "We knew an island once, Kori. But it wasn't this one. It wasn't the one back then either. It was ours. And it was imagined." She didn't regret saying so.

"We'll run your store," he said. "Together."

"Have patience with me, Kori."

"We'll care for your father. Until the end." He grew excited, the words coming out fast. "It'll be a new life. We'll go places." He leaned closer and his fingertips brushed against her hair and the string around her neck and she instinctively pressed her hand against her chest.

"No," she said.

He pulled away. He flipped through his notebook and she glanced at the cloud faces he had drawn.

"Kori," she said, reaching for his hand. There was time, she told him. He was here to stay. She asked for patience again.

On the beach the campers had grown silent, gathered around the fire. She brushed sand from her legs, then stood to go. They left the beach and returned to the coastal road. Once more, on the motorbike, she held his hips. The shoreline darkened. As they went faster she pressed her ear against his back and thought of swimming and listened for his heart.

That night she joined her father in his bedroom. Together, in the darkness, on the small couch beside his bed, they watched television. The blinds were closed, the way her father preferred. His face glowed silver blue and appeared much younger, smooth and untainted. She thought of Kori as an old man and then as a boy and she wondered what his father looked like, as she often did, and whether he was still alive and what it was he had done and how he had come to know Kori's mother. She used to think of all this during school lessons, or later, when they took their day trips, in the quiet hours when they spoke little, their silence another language, an altogether different conversation through which he told her: *I am afraid of myself.* And in her mind she held him the way she should have.

She took her father's hand. It was warm and soft and he

rubbed her fingers with his thumb, slowly, the way a blind person might read. They were watching a show with singers performing and the camera turned to the crowd during the songs, young girls clapping and old women shaking their hips and raising their arms. It was a show her mother used to watch, for the singing. Her father had bought her mother a karaoke machine one Christmas and she used to spend hours with the microphone. She was an awful singer. And Sojin would laugh in her room, covering her mouth, loving her.

She rested her head against him and inhaled his old smell. He had crossed rivers. He had once carried a rifle and saw faces that bled. He had run and shouted and wept. He had found love and raised a child.

With her lips close to his ear, she said to him: "You did all that was right. Know that it was of worth, if you don't already." And then she pressed her cheek against the side of his face. She wiped her eyes. He laughed at something on the television. Although it was warm, she pulled his blanket over him and tucked it under his chin. She shut his door as quietly as she could, leaving the television on.

For the rest of the evening she sat on the front step and watched the line of hills blend into the sky. The low stars. The lights above the street burst white as they came on, then flickered dimly. The brother and sister appeared, kicking a ball down the street. They spent every night out here, until their parents called through the windows. She hoped to watch them grow old.

Beyond them lay the fields and the forest that once caught fire, though she first saw the sky. It resembled the sun rising in darkness, she remembered, swallowing everything it touched. She heard shouting and saw through the window her neighbors running, the bare feet of a man who left footprints against the dirt, the tapping slippers of a woman. She rushed across the fields with her parents as the sirens approached. She looked for Kori. She watched the planes come in from the mainland and sweep by the hills, the firemen lifting their spitting hoses. Trees thinned, heat causing the forest to flutter. The sky was red and thick, as though it were slowly descending. She heard wood crack, the barking of dogs. The bystanders silent. The fire raged. It seemed the earth had opened to reveal the great mouth of a dragon. Kori, she wanted to say, but the words wouldn't come.

It was then a figure—a woman or a girl, she couldn't tell—emerged from the burning forest and onto the field, stumbling. And then the flames behind her turned into fingers, a hand, and it reached for her, hungrily, as though it had been wanting to for years. It touched her, placing a halo over her head, and the halo glowed blue and green, the woman's mouth opening, her coal eyes, her twisting shape. The length of her hair. The rush of firemen. Her father running. The sigh of leaves.

Sojin held her mother's hand, her body warm against the fire. The burning woman like an escaped angel. And although she never admitted it to anyone, she thought it beautiful.

She never forgave herself for thinking that.

It had been the pig farmer's daughter. Her dog had fled and she had gone looking for him.

Kori did not come to the store the next day. After closing and locking the doors, she walked home in the early evening, stopping at the country club to watch the golfers, the white flashes flying over the hills like stars. She walked beside the fields and turned onto her road, waving at a neighbor who was tending to a garden. A girl rode past her on a bicycle, kicking dust.

She did not go immediately into the house but stood by its entrance. Through the window she saw her father sitting on the couch, holding his cane as if he were about to stand any minute now. She thought: if she stayed out here in front of the door, how long would it take for him to notice she had yet to return, before he approached the window and looked out?

When she was young she had once watched him run the length of the field with the neighborhood children. She had been helping her mother in the kitchen. She did not know exactly what he was doing at first but then spotted the ball he was kicking through the grass, his arms gesturing high in the air, his body growing dimmer as he ran farther and farther into the distance. "Mama," she said, tugging on her sleeve, pressing her palm against the window. "Mama. Is Papa coming back?"

Now she entered the house and brought her father to the kitchen. At the table she sat beside him while he ate his noodles and she spoke of the shop. When he was finished she lifted the napkin from his shirt collar and folded it for tomorrow. On his way to his room, he said, "Someone came by for you today." She placed the bowl in the sink. "Was it Kori, Papa? Do you remember?" He looked at her blankly. She held his shoulder. "It's okay," she said.

She went into her bedroom to change. She would visit him. She had yet to see his home. For it was a home he wanted, the reason why he returned, he said, and perhaps that was as good a reason as anyone could give. Perhaps she was wrong, she had thought all day. She would tell him she had been afraid. He was too quick. Whether they deserved each other or not seemed irrelevant. There was history, there was that. In front of the mirror she imagined her naked stomach growing. She gave a quick smile at her image.

She opened her mother's jewelry box. Her hand jerked away, her body went weightless. The box was empty. She knew at once, though at the same time refused to believe it, the way it had always been. She reached for the string around her neck. The key was still there. Hurrying, she dressed.

The sun was setting. She pushed her bicycle down the road, the gears groaning and rusted. She pedaled up the hill, standing, passing the fields, the cows motionless and indifferent. She climbed as fast as she could, her neighborhood receding. She felt the pressure of the warm winds, the monsoon season approaching.

Kori's house, a one-story, stood on the slope of the hill. Two windows, their glass broken, faced the distant town. The front door of the house was boarded with plywood, a hazard notice nailed to it. She called his name, though realized it was useless. She went around the back. A stray dog licked the end of a rusted hose, then ran away upon seeing her. The rear windows were boarded as well. There was a space that a board didn't cover, near the bottom of one window, but she saw nothing inside. Dust colored the glass.

She pedaled down the hill. She rode into the woods where his mother's house once stood, though she could no longer recall where exactly. There were new houses now. In a small clearing she found a pair of socks and empty bottles but she couldn't tell how long they had been there. She looked for his tire tracks but found several, unable to distinguish the motorbike's.

She would have given him the jewelry if he had asked, she told herself now. She would have given him cash if he preferred it. She would have. When Kori left the island she gave him all her savings, which wasn't much, but enough for a few days. To get used to things, she told him, and then they embraced and she placed her lips against his neck. She did it quickly, without thinking, tasting the salt of his skin. It had been morning, early, the sun not yet warm. She waved to him as the plane sped across the water and lifted, soaring. He would have remembered it. He should have known she would have helped him again.

She never asked him where he was on the evening when the trees and his mother burned. He never said.

She rode fast, past the fields and to the town. The day was fading. At the country club she looked for him. "He was going to work here," she said to a man behind the reception desk. "Cutting the grass. He was to work the machines." They didn't know who he was.

There had been times when she feared him, knew what it was he had done. "You're imagining things," he might have said. And perhaps he would have been right. But even if it were true, she would have been quick to forgive. Because she understood. Because in fear there had been love, though she didn't say that either. She had said nothing, not to anyone. She had lived with that, she wanted to tell him now.

At the house her father was sitting in front of a muted television. The lights were off, the shades drawn. "Papa," she said, rushing to him, leaning forward. "Did Kori visit again? The man who came for dinner the other night?" She gripped his shoulders and shook him. "Papa," she said, and shook him harder, and he looked at her uncomprehending, his breath salty from the noodles he had eaten. He had not bathed in weeks. She shook him and he groaned, his neck craning sharply from her pushing.

She let go.

Her father's lips trembled and she could hear his breathing. His hands, in loose fists, rested on his thighs. He was looking at a point behind her. She sank to the floor and pressed her head against his knees. The room was lit from the television. On the screen a man was boarding a ship.

"Was it Kori?" she said one last time. She steadied her father's hands. His chin was damp with his spit and she wiped it away with her thumbs, brushing over his coarse stubble. "I will tell you about him," she said. "You will remember." She picked up his cane, which he had dropped, and placed it across her lap. She turned and sat with her back against his legs. "I knew him as a boy," she said. "And then he left."

Her father did not respond.

"He traveled great distances. He started fires."

She heard her father stir, his breathing slow.

"And I thought it beautiful. And loved him."

Cityscapes flickered on the television.

Her father, his chin against his chest, had fallen asleep. Sojin remained beside him. She felt the heat of the closed room, the bare walls and the shaded windows. The blue light. She waited, unaware that across the entire island there had been others before her and others who would, in the following months, find certain valuables missing. That he had made a life of this. That he had come not for her but for many.

Outside, the hills opened into night. The winds, like great birds, came in from the sea.

SO THAT THEY DO NOT HEAR US

THEY WERE KNOWN AS THE SEA WOMEN and she was one of them. On the beach, clad in a wetsuit, Ahrim walked barefoot toward the water's edge, carrying an empty cage tied with rope across her back. A pocketknife hung from a leather strap around her wrist. In her hands were a pair of rubber fins and a set of goggles. She walked with the gait of the young and her posture had remained straight all these years. She had, last spring, turned sixty-six.

Three of the women had already arrived on this morning and as Ahrim performed her stretches, she asked of their children and their grandchildren. They asked of her house and her neighbors. The sun was rising and with it the waves shifted in color, striped red and violet. Above them, gulls hovered in the air, taking the slight winds. Summer was ending; the monsoons had calmed. Soon the cold would come. There was a sense of transition in the water, the sand losing its warmth.

She liked this time best, the days in between seasons. She slipped on her fins and wished the others a good journey. She rubbed her fingers, as she always did, to bring them luck. And then together the women swam out to the sea.

When her body had warmed and she had swum far enough away from the shore, away from the others, Ahrim leaned into the water, kicked her legs, and forgot for a moment that she ever needed air. She dove blind. The sea was dense, constricting. Then the water cleared and made room for her. She felt it shudder. The ocean floor lay twelve meters below. Now eleven. Submersion and the world consisted of light towers, sunlit, and she swam among them.

There was the market to consider. What sold, what didn't, the time of year. Fresh mussels and clams, eaten raw with a spicy dip, seemed more popular during the spring and summer; seaweed in a beef broth was preferred in colder weather. She considered this, thought it through, sacrificed one for another. Octopus she often caught, in part due to her own pleasure at touching their bodies, their childlike gestures.

She stayed under for two minutes. Then the dizziness arrived and her vision began to blur. At first she ignored it, pushing herself forward, but her chest took over, caving. Pressure attacked the sides of her head as though a sea god were yanking her by the hair and she succumbed to the shock of it, straightening her body, her eyes focused upward on the aqueous sun. When she surfaced she sucked in air, too fast at times, so that she was suffocated by it, coughing, swallowing the seawater.

There was the common fear, each and every time. But always she looked down to see her hand below the water, clutching her prize. She had not let go. And always she dove again. She had done so for over fifty years now, as her mother did and her grandmother before that.

She went on until she was satisfied with her catches, her cage full, and only then did she return to shore. The others, too, waded to the beach and they gathered in a circle in the shallow water, and she joked with them, relieved that all of them had returned. They compared their catches and sometimes they traded. They spoke of the houses several of them were building with the money they had earned. They spoke of the growing tourism industry and the export business that had, over the recent years, provided for them. They spoke of profit.

They parted with a nod and a wave, "See you soon," and Ahrim headed to her blue pickup truck, where she unloaded the shellfish and the seaweed into iceboxes. She did all this with a deliberate slowness, waiting for them to leave first, watching the caravan of cars and trucks follow the coastal road. The gulls cast thin shadows on the sand and the women's footprints. She thought of the boy Sinaru and the news she would bring him. She thought of her husband long gone. From the horizon came the faint sound of an airplane's engine and she looked once more out to sea. The afternoon was approaching. She clutched the braid of her hair. The noise faded and the water remained undisturbed, bright and closed, as if nothing in a thousand years had ever reached the surface and broken through.

She was seven when she first dove, thirteen when she started it as a profession, helping her parents earn a living. At seventeen she married the son of a fisherman. This was in the time of the Japanese occupation, at the start of what would become the Second World War. One winter, during an uprising, they fled to the mountains. They slept in sheds and caves. She remembered smoke from distant fires, the speed of planes, a boy whose face was the color of crushed beets lying on the mountain passage, his legs frozen against his chest. Jinsu left on some nights with the other men and she did not see him until the morning when he would bury himself in her for warmth, smelling of wet wool, his body curled from the weight of snow.

The following year he was conscripted by the Japanese military, though to this day it was, for her, an abduction. They came for him riding horses. She clawed at their boots and the horses' flanks. They kicked her down and she hit her head against the base of a tree. Briefly she lost consciousness. When she woke, her eyes focused on the animals and their soft sighs, their white breaths. Hooves lifting, stamping the ground. Tremendous eyes. As if they had come from myth. And then Jinsu stepped into the view, bending over her, covering the sun and the leaves. "I won't be long," he said, touching her face. She never heard from him again. Her last memory of him was of the horses trotting away and Jinsu turning, trying to wave with his bound wrists. The white of his shirt, the dark of his skin. Her husband the centaur.

He was twenty years old, she a year younger. They had no children. Their marriage had lasted seven seasons.

This was over forty-five years ago. Ahrim never moved from their home, although the majority of her neighbors then had now left for the cities. She lived in a village near the eastern coast, by a road that passed through a field of forsythia. The house was a single room, its walls made of stone, a roof made of reed. Over the years it had changed little, except for the roof. It was now in the Spanish style, with tiles the color of wet clay. Behind the house there was a grove of tangerine trees that she and her husband had planted, intending to harvest the fruit and sell them. These days she donated the citrus to an orphanage or brought them to the city for the homeless.

She never remarried. Her and Jinsu's parents passed away long ago. A life was formed and she took it. Solitude came to her early, and these days it gave her little reason to seek the comfort of a man. The comfort of something, yes, but she did not know what it was exactly, desire having evolved over the years.

On her days off she took care of her neighbor's son after his schooling. Sinaru was ten years old. Ahrim could no longer recall how this friendship started, when exactly the boy began to knock on her door. His father worked in a factory that packaged fruit; his mother worked in a noodle shop on the outskirts of the city. They were emigrants, from a village on the coast of Japan. They had been on this island for three years.

One morning, when they were still living in Japan, Sinaru was swimming with his parents. In the sea they separated for a moment, and a tiger shark followed the boy. "I was caught," Sinaru once said. That was how he introduced himself, lifting his left shoulder, his arm missing.

He came to her this afternoon while Ahrim was watching television on her bed. She had, that morning, gone to the fish market where she sold half her catches to a man who ran a restaurant in the city; a Thai company bought the other half.

The child Sinaru knocked once, as was his habit, though Ahrim didn't answer right away. The afternoon light shone against the floors the way it did when she surfaced, the air always lighter than she expected against her, delicate.

Sinaru didn't knock again. He was a curious child. He was patient. He either waited until the door opened or, after five minutes, left and tried again later on. A minute passed before Ahrim found the energy to rise, rub her face, and walk to the door.

Today the boy wore shorts and an old T-shirt that was, Ahrim guessed, his father's. It drooped low past his knees and was cinched at the waist by a nylon belt. His left sleeve, empty, swung as he fidgeted. He had last week seen an American film about Caesar and had put together this outfit. His hair was cropped short, which made his face seem round as a melon. His lips were stained red from a popsicle he had been eating.

"I heard the bed creak," Sinaru said, looking up. Together they spoke a mixture of Japanese and Korean, the two of them having become familiar with each other's language in these past years. "It took you one minute to cross the room," he continued, calling her "Auntie." He smiled, showing where he had lost a tooth earlier that week. He slipped his tongue through the gap and made a farting noise.

Ahrim patted him on the head and let him in. The boy left his slippers beside the entranceway and then lifted each of his feet to wipe away the pebbles that had stuck against his soles. He took his time, balancing against Ahrim's doorknob to view the lines running up his toes.

"Footprints," Sinaru said. "When you see one, where are the lines? You see them on thumbs, you know. Like when you press them against glass." He lifted his thumb, as though testing for wind. "Did you find the sea turtle?"

Ever since Sinaru learned of the sea turtles in the Pacific— the ridleys, some as long as seventy centimeters and weighing up to forty-five kilograms—he was convinced that one was able to ride them. And every time Ahrim dove, the boy asked her to catch him one. He had already built an aquarium out of a large, clear plastic bin, which he had filled with seawater and aquatic plants to give the semblance of a future home for the creature. His plan was to keep it there and care for it. His relationship with the sea now came in the form of his imagination, brilliant and tamed.

"They're clever creatures," Ahrim told the boy. "Their talent lies in hiding."

"Did you find one?"

"They eluded me."

The boy nodded gravely, his expression contemplative. "It's the winds," Sinaru said.

Ahrim agreed, "Yes, child, the winds."

She offered the boy some cold barley tea, stored in a large jar in the refrigerator, but Sinaru declined, choosing instead to walk around Ahrim's room, as close as possible to the walls. He moved along the boundaries of the bed, the dresser, the stove. And wherever a shadow fell on the floor, he followed its outline. He stared at his feet as he did this.

One day she had spotted him through his bedroom window, dipping his head into his aquarium. He was practicing holding his breath. His hair, long then, spooled across the surface. Although it was customary for women to dive, she thought he was eager to learn. Encouraged, she asked the following morning if he wanted to visit the ocean. She described the jelly-skin of octopus, the cratered shells of abalone, the oily mussels. They could first practice by hunting stones. He grew silent, chewing on his lip, curling his hand. "That's okay, Auntie," he said, no more than a whisper, and she watched his eyes and never brought it up again.

Sinaru had circled the room three times already. He passed the bed and pointed at the mattress and the thin blanket, ruffled and flattened from Ahrim's body. "I see you there," the boy said.

The afternoon light was strong and it came through the windows, illuminating Sinaru's skin, the wooden floor, the steel of her stovetop, the folding screen beside her bed, the bare walls.

"I would like a room," Sinaru said. "Like this one. And have everything I want in it."

"And what would you want?" Ahrim asked.

"Water," Sinaru said.

He wanted a room filled with water. And sea creatures. For in addition to his fixation on turtles, the boy was also convinced that if you tried for long enough, the possibility of drowning grew less, until the danger altogether vanished. He thought Ahrim had accomplished this, no matter how much she tried to tell him otherwise. His theory was supported by her constant scent of ocean water and by the answer she once gave him when he asked why she dove: *because I have yet to die.* And so he believed her to be of another world. His conclusion was logical. "You are a sea woman," the boy said. "Then you are also a woman of the sea."

.   .   .

He wanted fresh tangerine juice so they walked to the grove behind Ahrim's house. He insisted on carrying the stepladder. He held it tucked under his arm, his shoulders stooped from the weight, careful so that the metal legs avoided her body. Instead of the sea they took walks in the fields and hunted fruit, the boy exuding a confidence in these places.

Some nights Sinaru's parents fought. From what Ahrim could hear, it consisted of bickering, mostly, about shutting doors and noise and cleaning. Oftentimes it was the husband's voice she heard, and she did not know where the child was when this happened. She asked now of his parents and the child shrugged. "Papa has headaches. They are very bad. He rubs his forehead and makes a face like this." Sinaru scrunched up his brows. "And sometimes I want to touch the wrinkles on his face but I don't. When he comes home I cover my mouth and try not to move around too much."

The boy opened the ladder and placed it against a tree, wiggling it to test its support. Ahrim asked if he wanted to climb but he shook his head. "My legs are sore," he said, and they left it at that. So Ahrim stepped up onto the ladder and the boy held the bottom rung, directing her on which tangerines to pick. He pointed and she chose them and slipped them into the pocket she had formed with her apron. She was surrounded by their scent, both sharp and light, the smell, she used to imagine, of the sun.

Solid earth. The boy's feet rooted there. He no longer

swam and he no longer climbed trees. As though vulnerability lay only above or below the ground.

In her years in the sea, thirty women had perished. Some vanished, the currents taking them over the horizon. Others bobbed up to the surface, their backs like miniature bridges. Very few were victims of sharks, as many assumed was the greatest fear in the water. It was, for the most part, the ones who overestimated how long they could hold their breaths, reckless and determined. She had known each of them. Just as she did the women who accompanied her now, all her age, save for one. Interest was fading, the girls heading to the cities.

Her occupation, over time, would cease to exist. She would be relegated to history, that old word she carried with her always, that feeling that there was a time from which she had departed and was now wishing to return to. She existed in the middle, always. But it was different, she thought, in water. For there, time was not linear. It was, in her mind, a globe, spherical. Death perhaps was less important in that space because it remained inseparable from the living. Within the world of the sea, all was enclosed, all was present. The ritual of burial and mourning seemed nonexistent.

"That one," Sinaru called from below, pointing at a tangerine some distance away. She held on to a branch and leaned forward. She stretched her fingers. She grazed it and the tangerine spun. She felt her calf muscles tighten. The boy urged her to try again. She did so and succeeded and she blushed because she was proud. "Happy?" she called, showing it to him. Its skin was smooth and she weighed it in her hand.

"You have a big bum," the boy shouted.

Narrowing her eyes at him, she dropped the tangerine onto his head. She waited for him to say something but he didn't and she saw him fall. He lay on the grass with his mouth slightly open, and Ahrim quickly descended the ladder, jumping the last two rungs, spilling her pickings. She kneeled before him. "Sinaru," she said, shaking him, patting his head. "Sinaru."

The boy, under the sun, opened a single eye and grinned and slipped his tongue through the gap in his teeth. Laughter erupted from within his chest and he squirmed under her grip as she attempted to spank him. He freed himself and, still laughing, ran past the trees, farther into the grove like some infant spirit, his empty sleeve billowing with his speed.

Ahrim did not follow him. He would return. She sat there on the grass and looked up at the looming fruit in the shapes of dozens of faces, tilting in the winds, about to snap their necks and drop. She felt an old sadness, the smell of snow and horses, and then her strange fantasy faded. But the feeling stayed. And she did not know where the years had gone.

The next afternoon, as Ahrim returned to the village, she found Sinaru's father pacing in front of his house. Every so often he slammed his fists against the shut door and shouted something in Japanese that Ahrim could not discern. He had a fine jawline, dark eyebrows, and strong, thick arms. Although autumn was soon approaching, he was sweating through his T-shirt, leaving a trail between his shoulders. Sinaru's mother could be seen behind one of the windows. She held a broomstick, the bristles of which she tapped on the windowpane, as though her husband were a fly she were trying to swat.

There were women who found him attractive, she knew. She had heard one speak of him to a friend at the market, pointing at the different sizes of fish, in mischief.

Ahrim shut off the engine of her truck. He turned and stared at her blankly, his eyes large and white against his tan skin. They were Sinaru's eyes.

He approached her, grinning. "Sea woman," he called. "Have you seen my son?" He looked at her as if he knew something about her and wouldn't tell—he always looked this way. He leaned on the passenger-side door and tucked his head through the open window. "I want to see my boy," he said. "My son."

"I haven't seen him," she said.

He smelled of cellophane, the plastic of the factories. He chewed on his fingernails. "Aren't you his play buddy?" he said.

"I'm sorry," she said. "I've been at the market all day."

He lifted his hands. "Sure," he said. "But if you do see him, tell him he should come find me, yes?"

"All right."

"And tell him to bring her along." Sinaru's father pointed his thumb to where his wife stood behind the window.

Ahrim left her truck and walked up the pathway to her house. She still kept her door unlocked, like the old days, and so she entered thinking perhaps the boy was inside. He would never, not when she wasn't there, but she thought it all the same and sighed when she saw that he wasn't. She went outside again and headed to the backyard and the grove where the scent of citrus lingered and the bark of the trees was bright under the sun, which split and shadowed along the leaves. He wasn't there either. She called for him, in a low voice, afraid that his father might hear. "Sinaru," she said. "Sinaru. Where are you hiding?"

When she returned to the front of the house the street was empty, save for a group of children kicking a ball in the neighboring playground, dust rising to their shins. The father was gone. Had Sinaru's mother acquiesced and allowed him entry? Had he left? There was his car in their gravel driveway. He could have walked, she considered, to the nearby noodle shop for a drink. He could be spending the night elsewhere. The woman had kept the door closed. It was what she would have done, Ahrim concluded.

There was dinner to cook, although she no longer felt like cooking it. She was tired. It had been the diving, yes. She remained in front of her door and looked out across the street at the varying roofs of the village, some of them still made of strips of reed. The light of day was paling toward the blue of evening. The weather cooled. She listened to the soft thud of sneakers scuffling along the playground.

She hardly knew her neighbors. There were younger couples now. It was likely, she thought, that they spoke of her inside their homes. Same as always, they would comment over dinner. Their spouses would shake their heads. They would look at their children, with assurance, in their silence perhaps a concern. *She keeps time with the young boy, a woman her age, her solitude.*

A few days passed. There had been an incident at Sinaru's school and today she waited for him.

She boiled seaweed. When they were softened she marinated them with sesame oil, rice vinegar, a drop of sugar, and some spices. She ate them in a glass bowl, cupping it with her hand, bringing the rim close to her lips, using her chopsticks. She sat on the floor, her legs crossed, beside the folding screen behind which she used to undress. Jinsu used to turn away even though the screen covered her nakedness. She would step lightly around the screen and surprise him, covering him with her hair, and he would look back at her curious and shy, taking in her body.

Not long after Hiroshima and Nagasaki there had been propositions. But Ahrim remained steadfast, convinced Jinsu would return.

There he was. She saw the boy through her window, crossing the street, and she thought that what seemed inherent in some was caution. She herself took it from her life in the sea, which moved and pressed against its environment in a perpetual act of provocation. She opened the door before the boy could knock and so upon first sight she saw his hand in a fist, raised, his knuckles pointing at her. He wore a different shirt, cleaner, fresh. Cinched at the waist this time was a long thread of twine. A stick was tucked inside it, the end of which he had sharpened to a point. His bruises were healing. The skin of the young did so, much faster than the old.

Two days ago, three boys had wanted to see his stump.

The first punch was to the side of Sinaru's head. When his body bent, they kicked his shins and hit him on the shoulders, and then ripped the sleeves of his shirt. "The Jap has a second dick," they said. They stole his belt, taking turns whipping him, then twirling it in front of their crotches, telling Sinaru to pull on it.

She had gone looking for the boys. But he refused to tell her who they were, and so, yesterday afternoon, she remained in front of the school building and searched the crowd for who had hurt him. She stayed until she saw Sinaru and then walked him home.

She knelt beside her door and examined his legs. The bruises there were the color of a mussel's shell, the color of the outer rim of stars.

"I made this," Sinaru said, tapping his sword. He looked down at her. He was filled with pride.

"Let's have a look."

She stood and he presented the sword to her. It was a branch of a forsythia, its golden flowers gone. At the sharp end its flesh was revealed, nearly white against the bark. He would have used a kitchen knife, perhaps, something a bit dull. She could tell from the unevenness of his cuts.

"I would like something for this," the boy said, raising the stump where his arm once existed. "I'd place it there and then I would be a knight and I could cut paths anywhere." He made swooshing noises.

"You'd rescue the princess," Ahrim said.

"Yes, I would."

"And would you rescue me?"

The boy considered her question. "You're too old to be a princess."

"True."

"But maybe I would."

"Here," Ahrim said, lowering the bowl. "Eat."

With her chopsticks she picked a few strips of the seaweed salad, twisted them, and fed the boy while they were standing at her door. She asked whether anyone had bothered him at school today. He shrugged while chewing.

When they first came to the island she noticed Sinaru's mother avoided looking at her son, the way she called for him by the door and then turned away. Ahrim remembered this, remembered the fear in the woman's eyes, or something akin to it, which, in the years that followed, turned into an indifference.

His father was like this as well, because the boy would grow to find his opportunities limited. She heard him say this once and she heard him say he wanted another child and Sinaru's mother didn't.

She fed the boy the rest of the salad. When he was finished, he wiped his mouth with his wrist and said, "Did you find one?"

The boy had missed a few spots and she wiped his mouth again with the tail of her shirt. She smelled his hair and felt the softness of his face. From her pocket she revealed a thin shell in the shape of a fan, the size of her palm. It was striped the colors of cinnamon and granite and ivory. She had found it at the beach this morning.

"Almost," she said, handing it to him, her gift. "I almost did."

The boy's eyes grew dim. She reached for his shoulders, to see the bruises there, but he stepped away. "You didn't find one?"

"No, child," she said. "Not today."

His reaction was unexpected.

"Then you're no good," he said, and crossed the street and threw her gift into the dirt. She gripped the door and in silence watched as he raised his leg high and cracked the shell and ground it into the dirt, twisting his hips, until the shell was powder.

. . .

Ahrim knew of only a few incidents involving sharks on Solla Island. The first occurred when she was in her adolescence, when on the weekends entire villages would flock to the sea, as though they had never entered it in their lives. Some were bold, swimming farther and farther, and although she didn't remember the man, what returned of him was a foot trailed by a cloak of deep red like some lackadaisical comet gone astray.

Ahrim was nearby when it washed up to shore and she remembered the tattoo around the ankle—which was how they identified him—an image of a swordfish, wrapped around the skin so that it faced its tailfin, the ink lines iridescent from the water and the sun and the blood.

Another was a diver. A sea woman in her forties. She survived it. Once, she showed Ahrim the scar that ran up along the side of her body, curved, like an albino root, where the shark had gnawed. "A pound of flesh," she joked with the tourists.

All sea women seek death, was a common expression heard among the island. It was a state of being almost there and returning from that place.

Her mother used to speak of the divers from fifteen hundred years ago. In those days there were thousands, the women providing food for their families. They swam without fins, their eyes naked against the cold water, and each time they dove, a bit of the ocean entered them through their open eyes and they took it back to their homes. For what? Ahrim asked. For their children, her mother answered. They carried the seawater within them and it surrounded the children that grew in their bellies. And the children were born and they were not afraid and they sought the sea.

After her parents' death, after Jinsu, too, was long gone, she would take walks alone to the coast. Hours before dawn she followed a trail through tall grass then climbed the walls of a bluff, and when she arrived at the high meadow she began to run, her eyes focused on the distant sea, stopping just short of the cliff's edge. She ran back and did it once more. All through the morning she kept running, over and over again across the headland until she collapsed in exhaustion, crying, blinded by the reflections against the far water.

Where she lay seemed to be the world in its entirety and neither the sea nor the sky existed. It felt as though she were being pulled into the white, and there was the desire, yes, in those days. Though it wasn't for death, specifically. It was the fall. To jump the cliff, to meet the water with such force that perhaps the world would shudder and flip and when she surfaced she would be where Jinsu was—that ash-eyed boy whom she met in the sea when she was sixteen years old, his fishing hook caught in her hair, reeling her in unawares as she struggled underwater to open her pocketknife. When she surfaced she grabbed his ankle and said, "You have my hair," and together they looked up at the clumps on his fishing hook, aloft, dark as kelp and dripping.

Years after the Second World War ceased, she would be notified that his body was discovered in the mountains of a Pacific island. In his chest pocket was an address, the one-room house on the eastern coast of Solla. The body hung within the canopy of a tree. They found him with his shoulders sagging forward and his Japanese uniform brittle, his face long ago erased of identity. It was assumed he had been propelled into the air by an explosion, though what killed him was the pointed arm of a tree that sliced through his forearm and then pierced his heart, growing within him, sprouting leaves.

On his wrist was a bracelet, which she buried in the grove they had planted, her own hair returned to her, a decade later, woven.

Ahrim was in the midst of a dream when she heard a heavy, echoing boom. She blinked and it faded in its density, like a contrail, muted and controlled. Waking, she experienced the familiar sensation of being lifted up from wherever it was she had been. Her eyes, focusing, revealed her kitchen. Her hair was still wet. So was her skin and she looked down and there was her body, naked, seated on her couch, her knees thin and wrinkled, her belly neatly folded.

She remembered now. She had intended to shower after coming in from the diving. Her chest throbbed. It had been a slow dive and she had gone deeper than she intended. She drove home with the pressure still pulsing against her skull, the sun sharp against her eyes. She had wanted to sit down for a short while and had instead fallen asleep.

Under her closed door she saw the pale edge of the afternoon light and two small silhouettes, shifting and unsettled: feet.

Someone had been knocking, she realized, and she rubbed her face, smelling the octopus she had caught. Her hands were numb and cut from the abalone she had attempted to pry off a stone. She pulled on a pair of shorts and a shirt from a pile of clothes she had neglected to launder.

When Ahrim opened the door she saw Sinaru and managed a smile before noticing the wound.

The boy stood shirtless. He had tightened his brows, as though in concentration, and his lips were pressed firmly together. His arm, across his chest, gripped his left shoulder. Below that was a stain. It seemed to expand as she stared at it, dumbstruck in her waking, as though the limb he once had was regenerating. Sinaru, with all his effort, returned her smile.

"Ahrim," he said. "I am leaking."

And then the edges of his eyes flooded and he leaned forward, still clenching his shoulder, and she lifted him and rushed to the couch and lay him there. "You're doing well," she kept repeating. "Just like that. Grip it tight." She ran outside to her truck where she kept her first-aid kit and returned and wiped as much of the blood as she could with a wet cloth before applying ointment along the end of the stump, feeling where the doctor had severed his bone. She felt the fresh puncture there, at the tip. She bandaged the wound as tightly as she could, wrapping the gauze up to his shoulders, asking if it hurt. "A little," he told her, and she wiped his forehead and asked him who had done this, although she knew already.

He didn't respond at first. He shrugged. And although it was warm she drew a blanket over his chest and tucked it under his chin, kneeling on the floor beside him.

"Was it the boys?" Ahrim asked. She brushed his hair with her fingers. "Was it the boys? Tell me, Sinaru. Was it them?"

His bruises had not entirely healed. And now this. He was alone, she thought. And they knew it and they taunted him and he did nothing because he was kind. He let them. He allowed it. Because he was afraid. Because his life was governed by an incident that occurred at sea, as though his days were a preparation for when it would happen again, embodied in a multitude of shapes and forms and places.

"It isn't right," she said. She clutched the side of the blanket. "I will go to them, Sinaru. Tell me who it was. Please."

The boy looked at her with calm and patient eyes, and he appeared much older as he took her hand in his. Her body shuddered from the touch.

"That's okay, Auntie," he said. "It was me."

.   .   .

Sinaru slept. She watched him. She heard a car idling on the street. And then another. After some time she left the house and crossed the street. The boy's aquarium, a large clear plastic bin decorated with stones and seaweed, lay in the front yard of his home. His wooden sword floated inside of it, its pointed end darkened by his blood, which fanned out into the stale water. She picked up the sword and slipped it under a bush that bordered on their property and then approached the door. The sun was brushing the rooftops behind her, sinking. A breeze carried the faint scent of charcoal and fire from the coast.

She was about to knock but hesitated. Through the window beside the door she saw movement, a silhouette. It turned quickly, like a coin, and then she saw the unmistakable sight of skin, pale and soft. She heard a woman's voice, muffled, the sound of someone trying to keep quiet. She leaned closer. She held her breath. In the room, against patches of sunlight, there was the lower back of someone, a man's, a woman's, she couldn't distinguish. Then a person's leg curved around it, pulling.

She should have turned away but she didn't, not knowing why. She remained there, listening, feeling her heart, and only when the bodies began to turn did she leave.

It was while retrieving the wooden sword that she saw a pair of boys watching her from the end of the street, their bodies darkened by the sinking sun. In between them was a ball they had paused in kicking. She rushed at them, flinging the stick, shouting, "Go away!" and they, not knowing what to do at first, stood there and watched her. And then they laughed, running. They called her things she had never heard spoken and they were much faster and ran quickly through the playground and the fields until they vanished behind the forsythia.

Ahrim returned to her house, where Sinaru remained sleeping on the couch. Shadows shifted across the floor, the movement of clouds. She took a towel and wiped his blood from his wooden sword. She watched his eyes flutter under their lids and knew that he was dreaming and she hoped it was of turtles and the sea and great distances.

In the evening, after feeding him, she carried him to the bath. The boy hooked the bandaged stump over the bathtub to keep it dry. She let his skin soak.

"Is it like this?" he asked, and she nodded, said yes, as he scooped water with his hand, mimicking a catch. "And the sea turtles?"

"As big as the tub," she said.

He grinned, satisfied. He was sure she would one day catch one.

"Let's practice," she said. To her surprise, he agreed. And so she counted to three and then he inhaled and slid his back down against the tub, the water rising up to his chin, past his mouth, his nose, until his entire face was submerged. She looked down at his wide eyes below as though his grin were a reflection, his skin breaking into ripples the color of the light bulb hanging from the ceiling. She saw her own silhouette.

What the boy was thinking she couldn't guess, but she watched him and considered then that perhaps she had been wrong about the sea. That it was not a globe, it was not contained, but rather it was without boundaries, in constant flux, and if you were in it without purpose, there was the sense of going nowhere and being nothing, the sense of insignificance. And that each descent and surfacing was a struggle against this.

She rubbed her fingers, then dipped them into the tub and flicked water against his knees. She wondered, as she often did, why his parents had emigrated. Whether it was the work or the boy or something else entirely. In all their time together they had never mentioned his country.

It was Jinsu who once said, before he was taken, that pilots, while in the air, held their breaths. In the mountains they had been lying in the snow, watching the Japanese planes in the clouds, their wings like glass, their contrails like veins. She asked him why they did so. Because of whom they are seeking, he said. Superstition. For luck. So that they approach in silence. She thought then of these air machines all of a sudden empty and soundless as they soared over the island. Jinsu pressed his fingers to her lips. They were not yet twenty, still children. But we hold our breaths as well, he added. So that we move quickly. So that they do not hear us. And she believed him.

Sinaru, still submerged, parted his lips. He mouthed words, although she couldn't tell what he was saying. A pair of bubbles broke the surface. She showed him her fingers, timing his submersion. Slowly, the boy shut his eyes. He lay motionless, the water clear. She inhaled and, in her imagination, joined him.

THE WOODCARVER'S DAUGHTER

IN THE LATE AFTERNOON, the farmers, while resting in the shade of a citrus grove, watched two figures ascend the hill forest. Some of them had gathered under a tree, leaning against its trunk; others lay in the grass nearby, their bodies heavy from the sun. They spoke little, passing around cups of cold barley tea and strips of dried squid wrapped in pocket handkerchiefs. When a wind came through the valley their straw hats, hanging on the branches above them, rose and fell.

They followed the paleness of two shirts, like candle flames moving along that rise of land. They watched as one would watch a flock of geese. From so far away they were unable to distinguish between the pair, unsure of who was leading, the American or the woodcarver's daughter.

It was the Yankee, the farmers concluded, for the girl as a child had broken her right ankle and the doctor had set it improperly. She limped from then on, unable to run or stand for a long duration, her ability to work in the fields hindered. Her marriage prospects as well. The gods, it was said, had passed over her. There was pity for the girl, though they kept it to themselves. Discomfort, too, because she remained reticent among them and, before the arrival of the American, spent her time alone or in the company of her younger brother. She did not leave the village often. She was twenty-three now, in the year 1947. Not yet summer and the monsoons would not begin for another month.

Her name was Haemi. And the farmers had guessed incorrectly. Through the forest she led, gripping the cane her father had made, the last one he would make, for she had grown as tall as she ever would. On the handle he had carved the smooth arc of a seagull's head, its eyes blank and worn away by her palm. When the incline grew steeper she hooked the handle around the trees and pulled herself up the trail, clenching her toes so that her moccasins wouldn't slip. In the humidity her pants, cut off at the shins, clung to her thighs, and her braided hair swung in rhythm with her steps.

Whenever she glanced at the young man behind her, she first caught sight of the canvas bag on his shoulder like some bright wing, then the faded pants of his uniform and the T-shirt he washed by the river. She listened to his dark boots against the earth, keeping track of the narrow gap between them. He could go faster. But he never did. Instead he pulled on her sleeve and cautioned her to slow. She would injure herself, he said, and she hurried even more, ignoring the soreness of her ankle.

And so they went higher. The air thinned and their breathing sped. The sun split like bullets upon them. They were surrounded by the conversations of birds. "Not far," she encouraged him. "Not far." And when the land leveled it came with an unexpected suddenness and almost at once she stopped, feeling her body begin to recover, the pulse in her legs, the swift beats against her chest, the lightness.

They had reached a clearing. From here the ridgeline was visible, touching sky. Down below, through the trees, she could see her village faintly: a cluster of thatched rooftops, lines of rising smoke, the citrus grove and the crown of a lone willow in the fields. They rested for a moment, facing the other side of the valley, and then she led him across the clearing, slower now in that immense quiet, following the curve of an outcrop until it receded and they stood before a shallow cave. Candles had been set near the entrance, some having been lit weeks ago and already burned, puddles of wax hardened against the stones. Farther in, they could see straw baskets filled with grains, their tops tied shut with twine. Pieces of silk, patterned in colorful stripes, hung from ropes. There were toys as well, and dolls made of burlap and horsehair, their shadows spreading against the walls.

She stepped inside first, over the offerings, heading to the far corner where there was room enough for her and the

American to sit. She propped her cane against the wall and took out a jug of water from the canvas bag, placing it between them. The air was cool and damp and she clicked her mouth with her tongue, hearing the echo.

In the thin light she watched him. His sweat had darkened his blond hair. Against his shirt she could make out the outline of his chest. She wanted him to react to this place in some way, a gesture, a word, but he didn't. He drank from the jug and she returned to his face, to its blankness which she had yet to grow accustomed to, his cracked lips, the hair on his cheeks hiding his youth. Twenty-five years old and he seemed to her much older, those years between them vast, foreign, and unattainable.

On the ground beside Haemi's legs lay a row of sticks, twenty-two in all, each shaved of their bark and the size of thumbs. She opened a pouch she had brought with her and placed a stick beside the others. Now there were twenty-three. One for every year of her life. It had begun with her father and when she was old enough she had brought the sticks herself.

The American extended his hand, formed in a fist. She unrolled his fingers. She could smell his drying sweat. He was holding a piece of chewing gum, and she slipped the gum into her mouth, savoring the sugars as they melted. She rubbed her ankle, knowing it would need to be soaked in cold water when they returned.

He reached for her leg. "Okay?" he said, in English.

"A-Okay," she said, and raised her hand and formed a

circle with her thumb and index finger the way he had taught her.

He pointed at the sticks, aligned on top of the stones like a bridge. "For the god," he said.

"For the bone," she said, tapping her ankle. "It is a trade. So that he will return it."

They leaned back against the cave, their bodies hidden from view. They chewed their gum. The minutes passed, although it seemed longer, as if this ancient space delayed the moments. From deep behind them they heard water falling. In the distance clouds moved over a high mountain. Their breathing settled; then the calm of fatigue.

He said, "Happy birthday," and in the shadows she brought her knees to her chest and they were silent among the silk and the dolls and through the forest came the fragments of an old song, a multitude of voices, and they looked down, as if from a window, at the farmers ascending the trees.

It had been two weeks since Linden Webb, the interpreter, came to them. The village—which lay within a valley in the central part of the island—had grown accustomed to the presence of Americans. The Second World War had ended two years before, and with the departure of the Japanese, another occupying army took their place.

Throughout that first year the American patrols were seen often. They drove through the village in large trucks, their fleeting faces hidden under helmets and sunglasses. As the months progressed the fighter planes entered the villagers' lives. Some of the residents paused to watch the steel bellies of the aircraft cutting through the morning sky while many did not acknowledge them at all, keeping their attention on the harvest.

The children began to expect them. If a plane was spotted they chased it across the fields, tracing its contrails with their fingers, and then they returned on each other's backs, their arms spread, spitting bombs. If a truck's engines reverberated on the dirt road they ran to the village entrance and waited for the noises to increase. They waved with shyness. At first the parents ran after them but the soldiers waved as well, slowing the trucks, careful, and in the visits that followed they tooted their horns and the children cheered. Some days the Americans dropped off sacks filled with canned meats, sugar, and coffee. These the villagers saved for the evenings, gathered around an outdoor fire.

Haemi, too, was often among the crowd, though she remained at its periphery. She sat between her mother, who knitted, and her brother, Ohri, who was not yet five. "Join them," her mother would say. "Leave me be." She pointed her chin at the children collecting wood and brought a hand to Ohri's neck to encourage him but he hesitated, looking up at his sister. "He's fine with me," Haemi responded, "but if you want us to leave, then we will." Her mother shook her head, pretending she had not heard. Nothing more was said until Ohri fell asleep on his sister's lap and their mother carried him inside.

On these nights Haemi waited for her father but could never stay awake long enough for him to come back. She followed his figure in the firelight, alongside the other men, and drifted.

Haemi spent the days with the work that her family delegated to her: feeding the pigs, bathing her father's pony, working in the garden, or spreading fertilizer throughout the grove. Small tasks, she had overheard her mother tell a neighbor years ago. "Poor child," the woman said, and nodded in sympathy. The villagers were pleasant enough. They said hello, asked how she was, thanked her if she helped around the other homes. To all this she responded politely. They let her be. For many, it was through her limp that they saw the lives she could have led.

She would have preferred to go with her father to the market, as she had done when she was younger, and lighter, but now the pony, a dark pinto, couldn't carry her along with the produce her father sold. She was unable to walk the distance—a two-hour journey—and so every week she escorted her father to the village entrance, her cane in one hand, the other holding the hand of her brother. Her father would bend down to kiss them both on the brow and say, "Take care now, be well," and she smelled his shirt collar, the scent of the garden, and said, "Be well, Papa, come back soon." She watched him lead the pony down the road with his shoulders slouched, his straw hat slightly crooked on his head, the pale smoke of his cigarette trailing him. She watched his weariness and thought of how far he had traveled throughout the course of his life. She stayed long after he was gone, as if he were still there in the daylight, the trees bowing over his form.

With her father there were days when after his work was done he placed his hand on top of her head and left it there as they looked out at the valley and she lifted herself onto her toes just to feel more of his palm. But there were also days when she avoided him, heading down into the grove or across the fields, when his movements were heavy and erratic from his wine.

As a child she used to sleep between them, her parents, sharing each of their mats. And when she couldn't sleep she watched their bodies in the dark. She saw them as mountains. She touched their faces, their hair, their fingertips, her mother's breasts, the scars on her father's body that had existed since she could recall, alien yet familiar.

She did not know their origins. "Money," was all he said, as a way of explanation. Years ago, when there was a food shortage in the village, a group of men had gone to Japan, her father among them. She was told they worked in the mines. Only her father and two others returned. This was during the first two years of her life. She had no recollection of this, though she often wondered if she had felt his absence as an infant and whether it still lingered, as if some part of him had yet to return from across the sea.

What she knew of those years was that she was cared for by

her uncle's family, her mother unwilling to rise from bed in the mornings. Haemi's birth had been difficult. Her father told her this once. He had found her in the fields one evening, the wine already in him. He said it in passing, unwilling to look at her, then stumbled into the woods. "It nearly killed her," he said. She did not respond, running her hands against the high grass.

From then on, whenever she looked at her mother, she saw this memory in her eyes and wanted to somehow take it away. Instead they bickered.

These days the child Ohri slept between their parents. Haemi took the spare room where it was once intended that she and a future husband could one day stay.

Marriage had once been a wish. But her brother was born and she took care of him and found happiness through the child. There was the balance of things, she thought, and considered herself fortunate for a companion. Nothing more was asked.

Some afternoons the children found her in the forest at the end of the village, walking alongside the river, without explanation, in apparent absentmindedness, her brother hugged against her hip. Casting spells, they said, with her cane. They believed that her mother had lain with a god, who, displeased, had cursed the woman. It was known that when Haemi was born it had been in the dark and so when she opened her eyes she first saw nothing but the shadows of her family. "Are the spirits with you?" the children said, under their breaths, when she passed them. When she was gone they ran around, tapping their heads, rolling their eyes, lifting their arms into the air like wild, intoxicated creatures.

She was unaware that they spoke such stories. Nor was she aware that it was her thirteen-year-old cousin, Haru, who started them. He lived alone with his father at the first house in the village. His mother had been Japanese. She did not survive Haru's birth. During the war, his older brother had gone to Tokyo to enlist. He never returned. After that, her uncle—Haru's father—kept to himself. Haru she saw more often, with the other children, though whenever she greeted him he looked down at her leg.

She had caught him some months ago watching her pee in the forest. She had been washing clothes in the river and was too tired to walk to the house. He was shocked by her speed. She caught his arm with the handle of her cane, her pants still around her ankles, and he lowered his head, turning away. "See all you want," she said. "Go ahead." She grabbed his chin and pulled him toward her body but he shook his arm free of the cane and fled. She watched the boy run and she did not know why she had done such a thing. She thought to apologize. She never did.

All through those weeks the trucks continued to appear in the village. They brought flyers now, too, though the villagers, having never learned to read, used the paper for cigarettes.

Whether Linden was on one of those trucks he never did say. But she would, all her life, remember that morning, at the end of spring, when he appeared. She had been pulling up a bucket of water from the well at the edge of the village clearing. The children saw him first. He came in from the road alone. Unused to an American without a truck, some of them ran away while others were too shy or afraid to do anything but stand there and watch as the young man walked past the village entrance. She searched for Ohri, then saw the top of her brother's head pass the window of their house.

She returned her attention to the soldier. He walked slowly with a rucksack strapped over his shoulders. He was unarmed. Tied to his wrist was a white sock and he held this up high, his hand in a fist. He walked the length of the road and stopped, close to where Haemi stood. She remembered the strong light of the clearing. Then the high ridges darkening. The swaying of water. She strained her arms to keep the full bucket aloft. His eyes were the shape of coins. Thin lips. The palest hair.

He approached the nearest house, Haemi's, and waited in front of the entrance. The children had by then returned to their homes. The door opened and with his eyes cast downward, he bowed to Haemi's mother.

She remembered, too, his boots placed outside, like a pair of abandoned seashells, catching an hour of rain later that afternoon.

He was given the shed behind the house where her father once worked and where they now stored the spare tools, clay pots, and the baskets for the harvest. Her mother pushed it all to one side and swept the room. She unrolled a mat along the floor. He placed his rucksack in the corner of the room and cleaned the shed window, long neglected, with his shirt and spit. It faced south, toward the grove, where the farmers paused in their work to watch him. The children came to visit, though they stood at a distance. Yankee, they called him, and he responded to it, waving behind the shed window, and they grew embarrassed by his acknowledgment.

It had been decided that he would work the fields. He joined the farmers on that first day and Haemi's father showed him how to fertilize the soil and prune the trees. He was a quick learner and worked with diligence.

Haemi's mother prepared him a dinner of rice cakes stuffed with crushed red beans and sesame seeds. He thanked her and walked to the willow tree, eating there. When he finished he washed the bowl by the well, left it at the house entrance, and then retired to his shed. In the evening the farmers prepared a bonfire and drank wine, Haemi's father joining them. She looked for the American but he did not return outside.

The next morning she awoke to find Ohri missing. She had woken earlier than usual, disturbed by dreams, though she could not now recall them. So she went to check on her brother, as she often did. When she slid their door open she saw her parents lying on their mats, their long graying hair unbraided. But the boy was not there. She hurried to the front entrance. A brightness surrounded her from the open door. She squinted, shielding her eyes. She kept silent, unable to call, although that was what she wanted to do, imagined doing.

Soon her vision cleared. The sky was pale and bright, the trees thick-leaved, the air smelling faintly of smoke. At the edge of the clearing a group of figures stood like the silhouettes of trees. One was tall with broad shoulders: the American. Beside him were the children, craning their necks and looking up at the man who now brought his arms behind his back, his hands closed. Haru was there, too, taller than the rest. A girl pointed at one of the American's hands and he opened his palm. The girl stamped her feet, choosing the other hand.

It was Ohri, in due time, who chose the correct hand. And once more the American opened his palm and offered his gift, which the boy placed into his mouth as Haemi watched, curious, leaning against the entranceway of the house. The game went on.

"Ohri," she called, and the boy ran to her across the clearing. They met in the path and she lowered herself onto one knee to embrace him and felt his body and the fabric of the shirt their mother had made for him. He smelled of sugar. He said, "Look," and craned his head back with his arms around his sister's neck. He had opened his mouth as wide as he could, the chewing gum on his tongue twisted in the shape of a pink worm and riddled with teeth marks.

She looked past him at the American, who remained

standing with his back straight, his shoulders brilliant from the sun. He threw a stone up into the air and attempted to keep it aloft with the insides of his boots, his legs kicking like the shadow puppets Haemi saw when the performers used to visit, their shows about the gods, the entire village gathered in the clearing. The performers departed at dawn the next day and she would wake to the rattle of their cart, filled with the desire to follow them down the road for a while. Instead, she pretended to sleep, forcing her eyes shut, until the sound of the wheels faded.

She clung to her brother and he squirmed, fixated on the American's game with the stone. The other children had formed a circle around the young man. "Sister," her brother said, though he did not continue. He said it and grew calm, watching the American kicking his legs. She rested her chin on his shoulder and looked up at the boy's profile, his dark eyebrows, his nose the size of a berry. She told him he shouldn't leave the house alone, that he should have told her— that it wasn't safe. He asked why. He said that she was asleep. "Then wake me," she said, and kissed him. "Promise."

The boy pointed at the American. "That is Linden," he said, rolling the "L."

"Are you now friends with him?" Haemi asked. She spoke quietly into his ear but he did not respond.

Linden missed the stone. He picked it up and kicked it again. The villagers were stirring; she heard footsteps, voices from within the walls of the homes. Her uncle walked toward the well and greeted her, yawning.

She told Ohri to go inside. "Be with Mama," she said, and the boy, without hesitation, obeyed. It surprised her yet she was also pleased.

In the kitchen she prepared a bowl of rice and vegetables. Ohri was with their parents and from within the bedroom she heard their mother's laughter, the boy chewing the gum loudly, the burst of a bubble. Balancing a pair of chopsticks on the rim of the bowl, she returned outside and offered it to Linden. He bowed, thanking her, and then walked to the field where he sat beside the willow and ate. The children scattered and she waved to Haru but he avoided her and joined his father at the well.

The next day Linden wasn't outside so she carried the food along the short path to the shed. She tapped the end of her cane against the old thin door and placed the tray at the entrance. She returned to the house. Through the back window she waited for the door to open. When it did she saw him bend down and bring his head close to the tray, as though he were examining the food, his long nose like a fox's.

Once again he ate as far from the village as possible. Later she learned it was out of courtesy. Except for that first day he would never enter her house in all his time here. Nor anyone's.

The third morning she knocked on his door and then went around to the side of the shed, pressing her back against the wood. She peered around the corner and when he bent down, his profile in plain sight, his blond hair hanging forward like the willow tree, she spoke to him. She said, "It isn't poisonous."

She was disappointed. She had meant to surprise him. She had already pictured the American's startled expression, his wide eyes, the sudden jump he would make, bumping his head against the doorframe.

But he did nothing. He did not even glance her way. He said, "You never told me your name."

His voice was unsettling in its tranquility. And although he had not perfected the language he was easily understood. She stepped out from hiding. She told him.

"And I'm Linden," he said. "Thank you. It is just right." And then he gave her a short bow and went inside.

She stood there for a moment longer, outside the door, listening to chopsticks and the wood of the floor creak.

It is just right. She wasn't sure what, in particular, he had meant. The food? Her name? She returned to the house. In the main room her mother was on her way to the garden. "Will you finally help?" her mother said, and Haemi apologized, following her to the backyard where they worked beside the shed. She felt herself blushing. She did not once look at her mother. If her mother noticed she didn't say.

The next day in the fields, as the farmers watered the grove, she worked close to Linden, always visible. They pruned the trees using machete blades. During a break he went past the well and took the trail to the banks of the river. From a distance she followed him. On the banks he took off his shirt, squatted, and dipped a bar of soap into the water and she watched as he washed his face, his hair, and his arms. His even shoulders.

She grew used to preparing food for him in the afternoons. She carried it with one hand. He sat under the willow and she waited, standing off to the side, leaning her weight on the cane, because he had asked her to stay. The day was bright. He offered her the meal but she said she had already eaten, that she wasn't hungry anymore, which was untrue. They kept quiet. She listened to him chewing and a wind came and pushed the branches, and their shadows stretched and curved.

He was never present when the American trucks came throughout the following weeks, though no one was ever sure where he was. It was understood he did not want to see them. As for his reasons they never asked. It did not seem to matter. Help was appreciated. They treated him no differently than any other migrant worker. He was respectful. He spoke their language. And to the children he was kind.

They were low on kelp, her mother said, and her father nodded, filling the sacks with vegetables. They were in the garden. The pony stood beside Haemi, dipping his nose into the open bags. Linden helped them.

"Just a few days," Haemi had overheard her mother say

the morning Linden arrived. "That's all." "He'll work well," her father said. "He'll do as we wish. And then he'll go." Her mother went outside without responding.

Whether her mother's opinions of Linden had now changed Haemi could not tell. The woman hardly spoke to him. And if her parents knew she spent time with him, as they must have, they never mentioned it. Sometimes the villagers waved at the pair, though some of them glanced away quickly, continuing to work. If there were objections they were not voiced. Other times her parents called for her and she and Linden parted and she hurried to help in the kitchen or in the garden, her brother occupied with the pony.

Linden now tied the spring cabbage with twine, holding one cradled against his arm and looping the string around the leaves to retain the moisture. They wouldn't sell as well as the winter ones, but each year they tried regardless. He picked dirt off the heads although Haemi had told him he didn't have to. She herself stacked sesame leaves that were in the shape of small spades and then she helped her mother place the soy paste into ceramic jars. Linden, unused to its smell, frowned, and so she placed a small amount of it on the tip of her finger. "Taste," she said.

"Don't bother him," her mother said. Haemi fed it to the pony instead. She returned and sat on a stool and twisted the jars shut as tight as she could. She asked her brother for help and the boy wrapped his arms around the circumference of the lid, attempting to turn it. "Good, good," she encouraged him, and pride entered the boy's face. These were her father's words when she herself was Ohri's age, when he spoke of her strengths. She assumed he would recognize the words but he kept his attention on the vegetables.

Beside her father, on the grass, was a rucksack filled with the wooden animals he had carved years ago, each wrapped in cloth. There were foxes, pigs, tigers, and several made in the image of his pony. For every visit to the market he attempted to sell them. He had sworn he wouldn't make anymore until they were all purchased and years later this promise was kept. Once in a while he gave some to the children on their birthdays. They called him the woodcarver because of these gifts, none of the villagers aware that he no longer pursued the craft.

The evening before it had rained and now its scent rose with the humidity already present so early in the morning. The sun had yet to reach the rim of the forest. The day had turned blue, its colors sharp. They filled two sacks with vegetables. Haemi's mother tied the sacks together with twine, bridging the pair, and Linden hauled the bags across the pony's back, which was covered with a blanket. The pony stirred and grunted and her father stroked the animal's mane and spoke to him. To his family, he said, "Be well," and he tugged on the rope and the pony followed, keeping his head down low to the path and the road. "Kelp," her mother called, and without looking back her husband raised his hand.

He passed the village entrance and was nearing where the road turned toward the eastern side of the valley. Smoke from a cigarette rose above his head in a thin stream. She hoped her father had brought a hat in case it rained again. She watched the pony's white legs and saw how the right pair moved as one and then the left pair, fluid as a watermill, and she wondered if the pony was aware of all the times he had traversed this route. She had known the animal all her life.

To Linden she spoke of the market. She recalled the potters and their ceramics and the stalls lined with shellfish from the sea women. The voices of the medicine men, hoarse and vibrant, the sharp smell of their teas and ginseng powders. The auctions for the livestock—the oxen, the pigs, the goats— and all the hands rising and falling.

She had not gone in years, she told him. She tapped her leg with her cane. A two-hour journey by foot wasn't possible, she added, repeating her father's words, though whether she believed this anymore she was not sure. It was unfruitful of her time, her father used to say as well. In those hours she could work the fields, help her mother. She could help him, she once said, but he shook his head, telling her he would manage.

Perhaps he was ashamed, she thought, although she didn't share this with Linden. Perhaps guilt still remained.

Her father had by then gone and she turned her attention to her house: its thatched roof and the walls of stone her great-grandfather had built, each stone carried from the hills. Her great-grandmother had woven its first roof, replacing it every year, spreading its parts along the field like a great blanket. It was a house intended to outlive them, and briefly Haemi pictured it abandoned, empty.

They entered the grove, carrying a newspaper filled with the last of their kelp. Dried, the strips were dark, like night clouds. She placed them into a bowl and with a pestle ground them into a powder. Linden held the bowl and Haemi sprinkled it onto the damp soil under the citrus trees, letting it seep. They walked the rows. At both ends of the grove there were tall evergreens, to decrease the winds, and she threw what was unused around the roots. She licked her fingers, stained dark, tasting the salt bitter sea.

She admitted that in twenty-three years she had never seen the coast. There were times when she forgot she lived on an island. It did not bother her, she told him. There was the knowledge of other things. She knew what time she woke by the distance of the sun from the valley ridge. She knew how to make her father meals when her mother was feeling ill. She knew where the soil was the best for planting new seeds and knew how much a pig weighed by the girth of its belly. She knew when the pony dreamed and when he had slept badly.

"We keep each other company," she said. "We do our best."

They approached the river. She thought if they walked far enough they would reach the ocean and that perhaps one day she would go there and visit the caves on the coast. Perhaps, too, she would be able to go aboard an aircraft and see the island from above, how large it really was. Or how small. Either one. It did not seem to matter.

"It would be beautiful," she said. "It would all be beautiful."

In the distance they heard the engine of a truck but she knew it was far off, across the river, and that today they would not be coming in this direction. Ever since Linden's arrival the trucks had passed through the village several times, bringing flyers and food. There was an interpreter with them and he spoke through a loudspeaker, telling them of news in the cities and on the mainland. When they left she searched for Linden. The first time she found him among the forsythia that grew in the southern fields. Last week he was by the river, crouched beside a large stone. She asked if he, too, had ever spoken through the machines and he nodded, his eyes restless.

"I should leave," he said. "Soon."

"Soon," he said often, whenever she was with him. She had grown accustomed to this response, no longer sure of whether he would, in fact, leave.

They stopped where the river widened, the sound of the rushing water around them. Above, the sky expanded in color, stretching out from the crest of the valley and arcing over the village.

By the banks Linden knelt and took out his bar of soap. He washed his neck and his face and then gave it to her and she did the same, smelling its scent of mint. She examined his features, which she often did, his eyes in the shape of coins. She could not imagine his parents or his home or his childhood because it seemed he set foot into the village fully formed, as though what existed before vanished in his wake. She did not ask him about any of this, did not have the desire to, and instead imagined that all his years were in constant motion. He had crossed seas and she thought of that, too. Not once had she crossed this river.

Before they parted that day, Linden went to the shed and brought out a new bar of soap. "For you," he said. She bowed and hurried inside the house, where she spent the rest of the afternoon in her room, the soap tucked under her pillow.

Her father returned in the late evening. He entered carrying two sacks. One contained the food for the family, including the kelp. He had not forgotten, as Haemi knew he wouldn't. The other was filled with what he could not sell. Over half of what they packed, the vegetables and the soy paste warm from the heat of the hours. She smelled liquor on his breath. Her father said nothing. He went to the well to wash his face and dump water over his head and then went to bed, his skin still dripping. He had brought a newspaper, which he always did, for the illustrations. She listened to him turn the pages.

Her mother, after storing the food, sat in the corner of the room and began to knit a quilt by candlelight. Haemi crept into the kitchen where her father's rucksack lay. She opened the flap. She counted the wooden animals. There were several missing. In their place were unopened bottles of wine.

Through the window she looked out toward the shadowed hills and the fields, luminous and silver under the stars. The pony stretched his neck. The door of the shed stood ajar. Linden liked the winds to come through, he once said, while he slept.

It was there that her father used to carve his animals. In the dry evenings of winter he brought his wine and for hours she could see the door outlined by the light of a candle, the glow spilling out the back window and onto the grass. Once, she went to him, no older than four, and she opened the door to find him shaving the bark off a thick branch he had found by the river. When he saw her, he leaned the branch beside her and with his knife he marked where it reached her hip, his eyes blurry and raw. He had cut himself, along his thumb, and the thin blood ran down the scars on his forearms, dripping onto the floor. He ignored the wound and she grew afraid and left him.

The next morning he woke her. In his hands, his thumb bandaged, lay the first cane he would make for her, to match her height, its handle carved in the shape of a pig's head. He presented it to her and wept, kneeling beside where she lay, repeating the words, "It is for you."

She grew taller and the canes lengthened. And every year her father used what was left of each branch to make the small sticks he would take up to the cave and leave there, one beside the other, realigning them if they had, throughout the course of the months, shifted.

It would be years before she went into the shed one night without her father knowing. She stood among the baskets, pots, and tools that were now stored there, a blanket draped across her shoulder, the window holding moonlight. The woodcarvings her father had by then discarded lay on a shelf: albatross, seagulls, and sandpipers, each the size of a stone. There was also a flute he had made for her mother, one Haemi attempted to play once, unable to produce the notes.

Her father's knife lay in the far corner of the shelf, the wooden handle darkened by the dirt of his palms. She opened it; the blade was rusted and dull. She ran her thumb across the knife's edge. Then she folded it shut and slipped it into her pocket. She carried it with her always.

Once a week, as was tradition, each of the families of the village prepared a meal and, after sunset, brought it out to the clearing where they gathered beside a bonfire and shared it. Haemi sat between her mother and Linden. Ohri raced around them. The children of the village approached Linden and offered him a sample of their dinner. He stood and bowed for every child who approached and Haemi teased him. "Stop it and eat,". she said, pulling on his shirt.

Her father, who had been wandering through the crowd, now offered Linden wine and sat beside him, slapping his shoulder. "Good, good," he repeated. Ohri, with caution, went over to his father. "My son," he announced. He passed the bottle to Linden and lifted the child and together they danced through the crowd, their bodies dark against the light of the fire. Haemi took the bottle from Linden and walked to the grass where she poured out its contents. The liquid pooled, reflecting stars, then vanished. She gave the bottle to her mother. "He won't remember," Haemi said. She spotted her father and her brother by the well and went over to them. "They're starting," she told her father. He looked at her, as if about to speak, his face bright and shadowed, but she took the boy and walked back to her mother and Linden.

Now that the performers no longer visited it was custom as well that at the end of the meal the villagers would tell stories themselves. They stood in front of the crowd, beside the fire, and spoke of legends that everyone was familiar with but listened to nonetheless.

These were stories of distant places on the island: the Bay of the Dead, called such because the caves on the shore were once the eyes of an ancient creature, the cliffs above them its skull; the waterfall where the kings were said to be buried, and the passage across the forest canopy, used by gods, to travel quickly from one village to the next.

On this night they listened to a villager speak of a farmer who, unable to sleep, hiked up a mountain. After he had been walking for an hour, he came upon a glacier lake where he saw a group of maidens descending from the heavens. With every full moon the gates in the sky opened and they came to bathe until dawn when they would have to return. Before their flight, however, the farmer stole the clothes of one of them and hid behind a bush. When it was time for them to return, one of the girls couldn't find her blue dress and so was unable to ascend to her home.

The farmer, appearing out of the bush, consoled her and took her back to his cottage. In time they were married. She bore him children. As the years went on, the farmer, in his happiness, soon forgot about her dress, which he had hidden in a chest. But she never did.

And so one day she asked if she could try on the blue dress and he, unconcerned, consented. Feeling the fabric against her skin she remembered all that she had abandoned and, taking the children, she returned to the heavens.

With every full moon the farmer visited the lake. But no one appeared. Instead, a bucket descended from the sky, tied by string. When the bucket was filled, it was pulled up to the clouds. It was how the maidens bathed from then on, high above the sky. The farmer never saw them again.

And this was why all the villagers used wells. To remind them of the man who took a god's child.

At the story's conclusion a single voice broke the silence. The sound was not unlike laughter, though it seemed forced, determined. Haemi watched as the silhouette of her father stumbled toward the storyteller, clapping. "Good, good," he mumbled, and jumped onto the well, teetering on its edge. The storyteller held out his hands but her father kicked him away, and while the village looked on in silence he circled the rim of the well. He had his hands in his pockets and was looking up at the stars. He said, "Where is the rope, where is the bucket?" He then grew quiet and stopped. He lowered himself and sat against the well and faced the audience. The glow of the fire touched upon his slumped shoulders. Behind him, the trees were thin as arrows.

Some of the villagers made jokes, others sighed and stood to leave. Haemi's mother bowed to those departing, not once meeting their eyes. Linden remained seated, Ohri asleep in his arms. He was rocking back and forth, humming, his gaze fixed across the crowd at a point somewhere above her father's head. He had been covering the boy's ears.

For the first time the American patrolmen exited their trucks upon entering the village. Linden had been with them for a month now. The engines groaned, sputtered, and were silenced. Doors opened. The men wore helmets and clean uniforms and as they approached the villagers their boots glistened, reflecting the sunlight. One of the soldiers, his fingers tobacco-stained, was holding a photograph. An interpreter was with them and he spoke on their behalf. He said, "Have you seen this man?"

Everyone shook their heads, returning to their work. "Please," the interpreter said. "Try to remember."

Haemi was shown the photo. Linden appeared younger and she did not immediately recognize him. Or perhaps it was due to the fact that she had never seen a photograph before. She looked at it, astonished, rubbing her thumbs against Linden's image carefully lest it fade. But there it remained, contained within her hand. He was in a clean uniform. His face was shaven, his blond hair cut short. In his eyes there was pride. The background was nondescript, a bare wall.

"Do you recognize him?" the interpreter said, who stood beside the soldier. The sun came through the trees and she placed a hand above her eyes. She shook her head. The interpreter asked if she were certain. "He was last seen in this area," he said.

"Positive," she said.

The soldier began to speak but she did not understand his words and the interpreter remained silent. They left her and walked around the grounds, continuing to show the photo. The children had been ordered by their parents to remain indoors. They now stood behind the windows of their homes, following the movements of the soldiers. From inside Haemi's house, Ohri, on tiptoes, gripped the window ledge and peered through the shutters. The soldier who held the photo waved, amused, and her brother returned it, lifting his short fingers.

The interpreter, who now stood in the clearing, began to speak to the crowd. He said, "If you are willfully participating in this man's escape, then it is a crime. If you are harboring him unwillingly, then please do not be afraid."

He went on. The soldier, standing beside the window, showed Ohri the photograph. The boy pointed at it. After a moment, Ohri formed a circle with his thumb and index finger. "A-Okay," he said, in English, and pressed his lips together to blow a bubble with the gum he had been chewing. Haemi hurried to them but their mother appeared from behind the window and took the child, disappearing farther into the house. The soldier sought the interpreter and words were exchanged but that was all.

They left soon after. The houses shook as the trucks returned down the road. When the noise faded Haemi carried Ohri against her hip and went to find Linden. This time he sat cradled against the arm of a tree near the river, several meters above the ground; his fatigues blended with the leaves.

"They've gone," she said.

"They stopped," he said, still up in the tree. "They got out of their trucks."

"Thirsty," she told him. "They wanted to use the well."

"It took long."

"Long time to drink," she said.

Ohri lifted his arm and Linden brought his hand to touch

the child's fingertips. The child made as if to twist Linden's fingers, as one would pick fruit.

"Harvest," Linden said, and descended.

That night, unable to sleep, she heard the voices of her parents arguing.

"It is time," her mother said.

"He works well," her father said.

"It's unsafe."

"He's been good to us."

"To her," her mother said.

In the darkness Haemi heard the unmistakable sound of skin hitting skin, sharp and sudden. Her body stiffened. She waited for Ohri's voice but it did not come. He had slept through it and she was grateful. "Sleep," she heard her father say. And then it was silent.

Haemi didn't realize she had fallen asleep until she was woken by the sun. She left her room to find her mother sitting on the floor, her head against the wall, the quilt spread across her knees, sleeping. For all the years that she could recall, her mother sat knitting every evening after the work was finished. For Ohri's eventual wedding, Haemi had all these years assumed. It was two meters long and striped with the colors yellow, red, blue, and orange. Her mother woke to her footsteps and, rubbing her eyes, continued her knitting.

"Mama, it's long enough," Haemi said. "You can stop."

Her mother shook her head. When Haemi attempted to take it away she resisted, pulling back, a sharp tug, and the quilt tore. They watched a silk thread release from the weave, falling.

Haemi stood there stunned; the silence deepened. She looked at her mother's toes, thick and calloused.

When her mother spoke it was as if the words came from a great distance. "It was how I counted the days," she said. "It wasn't for anything other than that."

Her mother set the quilt aside and went into the kitchen and returned with a wet cloth with which she began to wipe the floors. Her arms moved in wide circles and the wood darkened in arcs. She worked slowly and with care and Haemi stepped away from wherever her mother's hand swept.

Ohri was born when she was nineteen. Her mother was thirty-nine. Whether he was intended or not, she did not know. She, along with the doctor, helped her mother give birth to the child, the doctor aware of her mother's near-death nineteen years before. The infant's body was as shriveled as a prune, his voice as loud as thunder.

Because Haru's brother was in the war he and his father, out of respect, were one of the first to see the child. Haru, nine then, held the boy with comfort, as if he had done so all his life, tapping the infant's nose. Haemi remained by the door.

That night she was unable to sleep from her brother's

crying. She noticed her parents' door ajar. They had lit a candle. They sat beside each other on their mats and looked down at their new son. Quietly they shared a laughter. Her mother placed her head on her father's shoulders. It was the only time she would ever see her do this. Her father leaned down to kiss the side of his wife's face. In this gesture they appeared young, as though they had just been married.

For six months they would be seen close beside each other, like this.

If she ever thought of her parents as happy, she recalled this moment: how her mother leaned into him; how her father held the child's ankles and moved his legs. Ohri's cry, which they didn't mind then.

The trucks could now be heard all throughout the hours. They kept to this area and the surrounding villages. Though no one spoke publicly of their presence, the days altered. Caution pervaded the fields and the grove when Linden was present. The farmers no longer waved to him. They worked with efficiency and then hurried through their lunches.

"They speak of me," he said. "I should leave."

She called it nonsense and told him so. They were unused to so many Americans, she told him. "Stay," she urged. "It has nothing to do with you." They stood beside the shed and watched Ohri through the window of the house, following his mother. It was early evening, the citrus trees bright under the setting sun. "He is fond of you," she said, and all at once felt the guilt of using those words.

"You are most welcome here, Linden," she said, and bowed and departed for the house.

In the morning the patrol arrived in the village once again and everyone was told to gather in the clearing. The children were separated from the adults. The soldier who had seen Ohri approached the children. He held pieces of chewing gum. The interpreter followed him, translating his words. "Do you recognize these?" Two soldiers who appeared no older than twenty years of age stood at the center holding their rifles. The rest of the patrol entered the homes, one by one. They heard the clatter of kitchen utensils, mats being pushed aside. Dogs began to bark. The ponies of the village grew agitated from the pounding of the boots.

Haemi was holding her brother when he reached for the gum the soldier offered. "No," she said but the soldier had seen the boy's gesture and paused. He formed a circle with his thumb and index finger and raised his hand at the boy. Haemi reached into her pocket, gripping her knife.

She would never know why Haru stepped forward. But he did, in between the soldier and herself. Her uncle broke into a run, reaching for his son. The soldier jabbed the butt of his rifle into her uncle's stomach.

When the search was finished they took to the fields.

She kneeled beside Haru: a thin string of vomit dripped

from her uncle's mouth. "Go away," Haru said. She squeezed her uncle's hand. "Go," Haru repeated but she didn't and he gripped her shoulders and pushed her. She fell onto the dirt, dropping her cane.

Her father took her shoulders. "Let them be," he said, helping her rise, wiping the dirt from her face. He walked her back home. In her room he laid her on the floor and made as if to leave but she clutched his arm.

"Papa," she said.

"What is it."

"Papa," she repeated. She had grown dizzy, her father's body vague. She pointed at the cane with the seagull's head, leaning against the wall. "If it's broken, will you make me another one?" From her pocket she took out his knife and presented it to him. He stood there, looking down at her hand.

"Sleep, daughter," he said. He placed a hand on her head and sat with her, smoothing her hair.

He had rolled up his sleeves and as she drifted she followed the patterns of the scars on his arms. As a child she would shut her eyes and trace them with her fingertips. In that dark she imagined caves and him digging out of the earth, and she connected the pale shapes on his skin to form the stars and the air he sought.

She did not see Haru or her uncle the following day. Linden attempted to visit the two of them but was refused entry. He went to work in the fields, away from the others, finishing as soon as possible. In the afternoon the farmers, including her parents, met indoors. Haemi brought Linden food, knocking on the shed, but there was no answer so she left it by the door, pausing to listen.

When the farmers came in from the fields, Haemi took her brother to the river and bathed him. She found a place some distance away from the other children. Behind a rock she took off his shirt and his pants. She rolled hers up to her knees and took the boy's hand and guided him into the water.

"You stink," she said. She cupped the water and began to pour it over the boy's head. He closed his eyes. The water darkened his hair, flattening it, and ran down in clear lines along his face. She took the bar of soap Linden had given her and created a lather in her palms. She scrubbed the boy's hair with her fingertips and thought that if she did this for the rest of her life she would die content and know her life was of worth. She lifted her fingers up to her nose and inhaled the scent of the soap and she bent down to wash her own face.

It calmed her skin and she felt the cool of the river water bring clarity upon her surroundings, as though her vision had shifted. She began to undress. Her brother watched her, unashamed, curious. They had not bathed together in years. She heard the voices of the other children but did not care. They were far enough away. She took off her shirt, untying the sash, then folded it and placed it against the rock. She slipped off her pants, careful not to dip the ends into the water, and then took off her underwear. Her cane she leaned against a rock on the banks.

Naked, she stood there beside the child and laughed. Ohri smiled and she dipped the soap into the water and washed herself, slowly, her skin tightening, the pebbles under her feet sinking deeper with the pressure of her weight. She turned, said, "Ohri, scrub my back," and he did so, guiding the soap along his sister's spine.

She felt his hands and imagined all his years through those hands, growing, and she thought he would one day leave, she was sure of it, and her eyes welled and as much as she wanted to turn and hold him she did not. "Finished?" she said, but Ohri ignored her and continued washing her, over and over again, the same spot, she realized, between her shoulder blades, but she said nothing, did not tell him to move beyond that spot. She dipped her fingers into the water and brought them out fast, splashing her brother, and he shrieked and she did it again.

When she heard the footsteps she thought it was Linden. But when she looked toward the banks there they were, the children of the village, standing side by side, some with their arms crossed, boys and girls, like a chain of distant hills. She rushed to grab her clothes, covering herself, then wrapped an arm around her brother, bringing him behind her. She was shivering and she pressed her clothes to her chest as the water lapped her shins, the wind around her skipping.

"We were bathing," she called, and her voice sounded different, echoing against the trees. Her heart sped.

Haru was there and he stepped forward and picked up her cane. He hooked it onto his wrist and swung it wildly until it fell. He picked it up again. She watched as though time had slowed. She gripped her brother and felt the pressure of his breath against the small of her back.

Haru called to the other children. He said, "She is in love with the Yankee." He cupped his crotch and shook his hips. There was laughter. And then he climbed the bank. He leaned over the well and the cane hung for a moment, suspended, before he let go.

"Whore," he called her then, and when she did not answer he left and the others followed.

Haemi remained there holding Ohri against her back. She no longer felt the cold. It wouldn't be until later that she realized she had lost the soap. Down the river it floated like a miniature boat, growing smaller and smaller, and she wondered whether it had reached the sea.

For two days the villagers argued over what to do with Linden Webb. The majority, worried about future violence, wanted him to leave at once. But there were some who, infuriated by the American patrols, grew stubborn and refused to acknowledge such demands made by foreigners. He was their guest. He could stay if it pleased him.

Haemi avoided these meetings. Throughout this time she walked without her cane. No one seemed to notice. It remained in the well. If someone drew water she watched in case it caught the bucket but it never did. She kept close to her home, feigning sickness. Though he continued to work in the fields, Linden was seen less.

One night, when the village was asleep, she walked the length of the road. A mild wind followed her. She could not see the moon. The pain started quickly, stemming from her ankle and rising up her thighs and into her stomach, but she continued onward, to the gate, where her father left every week. She then turned and walked back through the village. Back and forth she went. Her eyes watered and she pressed her lips together, concentrating on her feet, pale in the darkness.

She did not blame her cousin, although whether she believed this or not she could not say for certain. The thought came as she approached the well and leaned forward and looked down at the stillness of her reflection below and the stains of stars and clouds. She saw them as the faces of everyone she had ever known and loved, observing this moment. She lifted her hand, like a departing sailor, and waved.

It began to rain. She walked around the house and pressed her ear against the door of the shed. She heard Linden's breathing. Across the yard the pony lifted his head, unbothered by the rain, but did not approach her. She heard the echo of an owl. The fields shone, striped by the falling water.

She opened the door. The room was illuminated by moon-light and his figure was outlined under a blanket, lying on his side. She stepped into the shed. He woke, startled, and she said, "It's me." He calmed and slowly she lay down beside him. Under the light from the window he blinked. His beard smelled of citrus and the river. She gazed up at the ceiling beams and the straw, listening to the soft thud of raindrops. "This was once my father's," she said, tapping the wall. The night came through the window in the shape of a wing. "Linden," she said, pointing outside. "There is heaven."

He craned his neck, following her finger. "That's right," he said.

"There's the rope and the bucket. There's the water."

He gave her half the blanket. The rain was light yet persistent, like the soft beating of drums, and she thought of those days when her mother came here when her father was away at the market. She would examine the wooden animals on the shelf and then, looking out the window, as if checking to see if anyone were watching, she would pick up the flute. For hours she sat in the privacy of this room and shyly raised the instrument to her lips. She placed her fingers against the holes and the melody came out quiet and thin and out of tune. But she played on, her back straight, sun on her brow. Her body swaying like the slowest of pendulums.

Her mother performed all the songs she knew and invented her own, and Haemi would sit outside against the shed wall, under the back window, and listen. With her good leg Haemi tapped the earth, matching her mother's rhythms, pretending it was possible for her to dance. She stayed long after her mother returned to the house, facing the field, the trees across the way unmoving. The bright hats of farmers. The rush of river water. Birds through the valley. Some days thunder from faraway, the reverberations of the Pacific Ocean adjusting to a bomb. Japan on fire. And yet, before her, this changeless scene. And what world did her mother travel to on those evenings? What voice was there in music?

She had never asked why Linden had run away. He had never asked what happened to her. Neither of them moved, lying beside each other on the shed floor underneath the blanket. The room darkened and the rain fell, blurring the window.

She spoke quietly: "It was a fall. I used to think my father was a tree. I climbed onto his shoulders and climbed down his back. He carried me all through the valley like this. We scaled rocks. We followed the ridges. 'Higher,' he would say, the liquor on his breath. 'Higher.' I stood on his shoulders. I reached for clouds. One day he stumbled over a crevice and dropped me from a great height. I landed on my right foot. I heard the snap. When I opened my eyes my father's body covered me like a tent and the world shook and he was running."

The moon had appeared again. Linden did not speak. He had pulled the blanket up to his chin. His eyes were closed, his lips parted, and she lay there watching the clear reflections of water swim across his face and the fabric, memorizing the patterns.

"Linden," she said. "I am sorry. But you must go."

She stood, wincing, and limped to the shed door. She said she would accompany him tomorrow. She would take him to the sea. And then she left.

She woke before the light of morning. In the kitchen, in the dark, she prepared a stew her parents enjoyed during the summers. She worked quickly, letting it simmer with the garden vegetables. She took for herself a spare carrot and a shoulder bag filled with rice, fruit, and strips of dried squid. Her leg throbbed and she dipped a cloth into cold water and wrapped it around her ankle. In her parents' bedroom she bent to touch her mother's shoulder. "Mama," she said. "There is food in the kitchen." She pressed two fingers against her own lips and transferred a kiss onto Ohri's, thinking how much the boy would miss the American and what she would tell him.

Outside, the air was damp and cool. The rain had ended, replaced by an early mist. All the windows were shuttered. The sky was a dim shade of blue. She walked around to the shed. The pony approached her, fluttering his lips to the carrot she held up to his mouth. The door of the shed stood ajar. In the same moment she knew, and did not go inside.

Hurrying, Haemi used a stepladder to climb on top of

the pony's back. She stroked his mane and spoke to him and clicked her tongue. With some effort she pressed her legs against his sides. He moved forward, following the footpath around the house and out onto the clearing. On instinct he turned to face the village gate but she pulled hard on his mane and the pony turned again toward the grove.

They moved through the low mist, under the bright remnants of stars. At the edge of the field, where the forest began, the animal hesitated. Again she pressed her legs together, the pain rising to her waist, and he entered the trail and began to climb the hill. She concentrated on his hooves striking the dirt. She leaned against him to avoid the branches.

In this way they ascended the hill forest. Behind her the village was waking, the farmers walking out to the fields where the trees seemed no bigger than shrubs, lined in even rows, a giant's garden. The winds were strong and she gripped the pony's mane. They climbed as fast as the animal could go, the forest canopy beginning to pale.

The cave did not appear to be where it had always been. Instead, through the mist, she saw a cluster of trees blocking the way, their thin branches at varying angles, some pointing at the sky, others parallel with the ground, and still others drooping down. She halted.

Then the trees moved. It was as though they beckoned to her, stepping aside for her to enter. She comforted the pony as she slowly approached and the trees turned into men, their dark clothes now distinguishing themselves from the leaves of the forest.

Behind them she could see the cave where the offerings were kept. The baskets lay scattered on the ground, overturned, the grains lying in a heap and spilling over the entrance. The men kept silent, looking at her and the pony with indifference. They wore thick belts, a shade of green that was lighter than their uniforms. They carried rifles. One of them tossed a handful of dried fruit into his mouth; another had taken a piece of white silk from the cave and wrapped it around his head.

In the middle of them stood Linden Webb. His face was bruised and blood dripped from his nostrils and mouth, staining the shirt he wore on the day he came to the village. He lowered his head; two men kept their weapons aimed at him.

The soldier wearing the silk patted the pony's flank, his hand brushing her leg, and spoke. She did not understand him. In the early light his face shone, his nose flat and crooked, as if he had broken it long ago. The silk was knotted at the back of his head and the loose ends flowed past his shoulders. He moved the way she thought spirits did, with a careful slowness. It seemed he was waiting for her to reply but grew impatient and rolled his eyes.

He motioned for her to dismount. She stumbled, limping back toward the pony. When she turned to face him he was staring at her body and the wet cloth around her ankle. He moved closer. She focused on the trees behind him. Heard his breathing.

Gently he lifted the braid of her hair, his knuckles grazing her ear, and removed the bag from her shoulder. He inspected its contents, then, satisfied, gave it to the nearest man.

He twirled his finger around the side of his head. He pointed at Linden. He twirled his fingers again. "Do you understand?" he said, and then in her language he said the words for "sickness" and "patient."

He looked at her once more, whistled, and then left the clearing. The others followed. They were young and their steps betrayed fatigue. They passed her and the pony without speaking, sweat and dirt streaked across their cheeks from trying to wipe it all away.

And Linden. When he approached her their eyes met briefly. She called to him. And then she stepped forward to embrace him, and as their chests touched she took her father's knife and slipped it into his shirt pocket.

If he noticed he made no sign of showing it. She would never know if it served him in some way. He walked away. Soon, as the distance between her and the men increased, she could no longer tell them apart. She remained motionless. The pony picked grains. The blood on her shirt and fingers began to dry. Daylight appeared above the valley and spread across the distant ridge, where a group of silhouettes were walking, it seemed, along the edge of a continent. She followed their course and imagined the sea beside them until at last their shadows fell and they were gone.

LOOK FOR ME IN THE CAMPHOR TREE

ON THE DAY MIHNA'S FATHER sold their farm and
the land surrounding it, the child kneeled on top of the bed
she had slept in all these years and pressed her nose against the
cold windowpane. Her breath fogged the glass in bright rings,
then receded to a small point in the shape of her open mouth.
It was winter and the first snow had already settled along the
hills and in the woods, dimming the trees. Hoofprints littered
the fields where the ponies grazed and among those lay the
narrow path her father had made to be with them.

Overnight, icicles had formed above the front entrance of
the house and it was there a man was now taking leave of her
father. He had visited several times over these past months.
Whenever he greeted her, he bent down to pat her head and
Mihna felt the urge to wash her hair afterward, although his
fingers were as clean as polished silver. A businessman, her
father had said. He was short and carried a briefcase. He wore

159

tweed suits and, even in this weather, wiped his forehead with a handkerchief, which he then tucked inside his jacket pocket. He was courteous with her father and as they parted, he bowed and shook hands with him.

Today seemed no different than any of his previous visits. After they said their goodbyes, however, her father did not call to her as he usually did. In these winter months the light faded before suppertime but it was early still, not yet afternoon, the sky clear, the sun the color of ivory. The car descended the hill, leaving clouds of engine exhaust across the fields, and her father remained there in front of the door as if he had spent the night in that position.

The ponies had yet to raise their heads, huddled under the wide shade of the camphor tree. Save for the occasional escape, having somehow learned to unlock the gate that led into the forest, they stood in the fields all throughout the day, sifting the snow and chewing on the frozen grass. Riders had been scarce in this season, though a few couples paid for lessons and rode across the grounds. The ponies were obedient in those times, their hooves flicking arcs of powder as they followed one another. Every day, at dusk, her father led each of them back down to the stable, emptying the field, where the snow blazed copper under the setting sun.

She used to accompany him and hold the lead rope, her father beside her, encouraging. "Guide them with your elbow," he said. And from the far hill, on the neighbor's farm, she heard the cows, a deep song, as though it came from the bottom of the sea.

But it had been weeks since she had done so, her father working alone. "You won't be with me now?" he said the night before, as he visited her in bed. She didn't know how to respond, feigning sleep. His hand touched her cheek and then he left, leaving the door ajar, as he always did. When her father was asleep, Mihna stood with all the intention of going to him. "I am sorry, Papa," she wanted to say, but she didn't leave the room. She remained on the edge of the bed, her toes unable to move from the floor, and she cried, pressing her fingertips against her closed eyes.

It wasn't a new life, she told herself. It wouldn't be any different. He had said as much. He had called for her, she remembered, several months ago, while she was listening to the radio, the way she did after dinner, listening to the songs and the stories that were on every Friday. "The Fox and the Maiden," was the story on that evening, when her father knocked. "Mihna," he said, "Come here." He picked her up, which he hadn't done in a year, Mihna too big, too old, as her mother used to say, and she rested her chin on his shoulder as he carried her down the hallway. She was wearing her striped pajamas, the ones she had begged her father to purchase at a department store because they resembled the clothes a prisoner wore in an American movie she had seen.

She sat where she did every night beside the dining table,

where her mother once sat, to his left. Her hair, unbraided in the evenings, shone dark against the setting sun. She had her mother's hair, it was often said, and her worried eyes. From her father she had inherited his small nose, his pointed chin, and his gentleness. Mihna was not yet nine.

"I'm so sorry, Mihna," her father said.

He was selling the farm. He had decided. He had tried, her father continued. He had done all that he could. He could no longer manage it, the house itself too large for the two of them alone. A smaller place was what they needed, he said. They would find a house close by. He had thought of her school, considered her friends, the ponies also. He would still run the stable. That was all arranged by the man whose hotel was to be built. He would give lessons for the tourists.

How long they were there beside the table Mihna couldn't remember.

"Say something," her father said. "Please, Mihna. Say whatever you want."

She had been staring at her father's hands, old and brittle. She looked away. She thought she had been helping with the farm, she wanted to say. For a year now she had been doing so. But instead she told him she understood and then asked if she could return to the radio.

"You don't have any questions?" he asked.

"The Fox and the Maiden," she said, knowing she had missed it.

But once in the bedroom she listened to the radio regard-less, searching the stations. She lay in bed and turned the volume down so that the songs murmured. She pressed her ear against the speaker. From behind the walls came the familiar sounds of the house. Against the rooftop, the ice shifted like frightened mice. The heating pipes sighed.

The days passed and her father packed and took breaks by marking the real estate listings in the newspaper.

There was recess at her school, for the winter, and Mihna remained outdoors in the afternoons. She stayed with the ponies, smelling the camphor on their coats, and if she heard her father approach, she took the trail that led into the woods where she listened to the chatter of birds, the soft tap of her shoes against the snow and the wet leaves. Among the evergreens the air smelled sweet, like the house after her mother bathed, and recalling this, she blushed.

Each day she walked until she reached a cliff that overlooked a small clearing below. Across the expanse the forest continued and far beyond stood the peak of Tamra Mountain, set between clouds. The trail sloped to her left and there, at the bottom, beside a small boulder, she collected snow in her gloved hands and built a miniature snow house. She spoke aloud as she did so, pretending she was the narrator on the radio, or sang the songs she had learned from her mother.

And it was on one of these days, not long after the businessman left the farm, that the ground ahead of her, in the clearing beyond the trees, flickered for a moment. Perhaps it was a deer or a fox, she thought. Perhaps it was simply the snow that had begun to fall just then. Mihna did not move, watching.

What she soon identified, however, were the glimpses of a body, split in her vision by the trees: a woman's head, her hair frozen, curved like a shell. She was recumbent, supporting herself on her elbows, and Mihna at first thought she was dead. But then the woman's breath rose in puffs, clouding her face. Her arms were translucent, like smoke. She wore a sleeveless dress with a sash tied around her waist. The dress was a pale blue, like the one her mother wore in a photograph Mihna kept on her dresser.

But the woman was not her mother. She was not a woman Mihna had ever seen. And either in shyness or fear, perhaps both, Mihna turned and ran up the trail and through the forest, leaving her snow house unfinished. A branch stung her cheek but she continued to run until she returned to the fields, where the ponies, unchanged, were sniffing the leaves of the camphor tree.

At the edge of the woods, by the gate, she waited for her heart to slow. Her father, on the crest of the hill, was heading toward the stable below. He did not see her. He walked slowly and when a wind swept through, clutching his body, he seemed unbothered by it.

. . .

A year had passed since Mihna's father buried his wife beside her parents, at the base of a small mountain in the central part of the island. Her heart had failed her, sudden in its departure, although in retrospect she had for days complained of dizziness, a slight pain in her chest. "You're overworked," he had said, on the last morning they awoke together. "Sleep a little longer."

It was after her death that the ponies, all of them, began to gather beside the tree she adored, through the seasons, searching for the scent of her hair, which they had grown used to, licking her braid and tugging at it whenever she fed them.

For three decades they had been married. A month they had known each other before then. Nara was twenty-four when Linn proposed to her. Linn was two years older. The farm, once his parents', had not changed since. "You are kind," she said, accepting. It was kindness one remembered above all else, she added.

The child was unexpected, Nara already in her forties by then. For years they had tried, and with it grew the belief that parenthood wasn't intended. But she became pregnant and when she told him, she pointed up at the ceiling of their bedroom. "A god must have tripped," she said, referring to the folk tale. "And out fell from his pocket a stone."

In that first week after her mother had gone, Mihna wouldn't speak, covering her ears when the ponies whinnied. She stayed in her bedroom and listened to the radio. Her father brought meals to her and they both ate on the floor, their backs leaning against her bed. He spoke of his day and asked of hers, knowing she wouldn't answer. In their solitude he felt the fatigue of silence, as though his body were being stripped, bit by bit, and he knew not how he came to be on this farm. He slept little, staying on his side of the bed, the other half untouched.

Though he must have slept, for one night he was awoken by a hand stroking his hair and for a moment he thought it was his wife's. But it was Mihna's, that hand connected to a child's arm, her shape taking form in that darkness, her hair sweeping across his chin. "Papa," she said. "I'm all right now." And then she left, shutting the door, and, thinking it a dream, he returned to sleep.

The next morning, she began to speak, as if she had been doing so all along. "When I woke," she said. "I said hello to Mama. Will you say hello?"

In her voice lay what he believed was the beginning of acceptance and the rhythm of the farm returning and he nearly cried out of relief and an exhaustion that he had only now recognized. She helped with the ponies, walking with him before school and then again in the evening before suppertime. She cleaned the stable and at the house she sat beside him on the couch as they watched the television or read magazines. He cooked for the child, steamed buns filled with sugared beans, the way her mother had done, picturing Nara's hands and the ingredients she used, how the flour caught under her fingernails and how he had cleaned them with a toothpick, holding her palms.

Before bed on Saturdays, they rode the ponies in the dark, through the trails, guided by the moon, something they used to do on occasion in secrecy, as Mihna's mother never allowed it. He recalled the mischief of this, and realized he expected Nara to be waiting for them at home, frowning. He would shrug sheepishly, winking at his daughter. But none of that occurred, and when they approached the house he saw the shutters closed and behind its walls an emptiness, contained, and the desire to enter it lessened.

The months continued in this way, with more effort than he understood. There was not so much her memory but the memory of her death and it clung to him and the house and the grounds like ash. Still troubled during sleep, he waited for the bedroom to brighten with the morning. He had done nothing with her clothes, her shoes placed by the front entrance from the last time she touched them, her toothbrush still above the bathroom sink, her soaps as well. Her scent remained in the closets and, like some slow poison, he began to grow nauseous from it and kept the door shut. The clothes he wore—a handful of shirts and pants—were slung onto the backs of chairs.

"It's so quiet," he told Mihna one evening, standing and pacing the living room. He went to open the door and let the cold air embrace him as he watched the hills darken and above them a pair of clouds wrap around the moon.

"You like the quiet," his daughter said. "You said so yourself. You always liked it."

It was true. Born here, he knew no other home, no other sound but what he heard among the fields and inside this house.

"Mama liked it, too," Mihna said.

Did she? he thought. He was no longer sure. The house had become foreign to him, indistinct, and no longer shared. He began to notice parts of it he had not seen in what seemed to be years. There was a specific corner of the living room where a bookstand stood, the open pages of his father's calligraphy book yellowed by sun. A particular drawer in the kitchen where his wife had saved coupons, now long expired, from the city's supermarket. The linen closet, with bed sheets he didn't know they owned.

His childhood, too, seemed to have occurred elsewhere, his parents' home envisioned in another town, another island, perhaps, one from which he had left. This sensation, in particular, intensified throughout the weeks, as if he had been traveling all this time and only now felt the longing to return home.

It was six months after his wife's death that Linn, late at night, rummaged in his desk drawer and found a business card with the company logo of a hotel on the top left corner, a name at the center. It was well past office hours, he knew, and he wasn't expecting anyone to answer. He listened to the telephone ring, imagining a dark office in the city. He hung up. He called again. He did this several times. He listened to the man's recorded voice over and over again. The man had approached him years ago, offering a generous price for the land. They would keep the ponies, he promised. For the tourists. Linn could provide lessons. The house, however, would be razed. A golf course would be built, the hotel overlooking it.

Linn left a message, inviting the man to visit the farm. And then, checking to be sure Mihna was asleep, he went into the kitchen and placed the leftover buns onto a paper plate. As quietly as he could, carrying the plate, he stepped outside.

On that night, guided by a flashlight, Linn walked down the hill. The stars shone, domed above the horizon, the silhouette of the forest like the shadows of flames. He raised his flashlight up toward the sky and watched the beam fade. He heard the scuffing of hooves as he approached the stable, their movements caused by curiosity, an unexpected visit, the sound of boots cracking the snow. He paused, turning to gaze at the glowing windows of the house, and he imagined each room connected not by a single hallway but a vast and intricate maze, the corridors shifting, he and Mihna and everyone who had ever lived there hidden and separate, asleep and in dreams.

A pony whinnied and he entered the stable, turning off the flashlight so as not to frighten the animals. The doors groaned and moonlight came with the wind, covering the aisle and the silver eyes of the ponies that widened with eagerness. He greeted them with a low muttering, as he had done since childhood, petting each of them between the ears and thinking then of his own father whose entire body appeared calloused, like the bark of a tree, but you would never know it from his embrace. He longed for the man and felt his chest grow heavy, for with the tiredness of these past months came not the sensation of aging but its opposite: he was a child and the world unknowable.

The ponies craned their necks, having caught the scent of the buns, and he laughed quietly and spoke to them, his voice echoing off the beams of the roof. And then, with a waiter's flourish, he lifted the top plate to reveal the food and began to tease the animals, lowering the plate and passing it underneath their noses. The ponies grew agitated, spiking their heads in the air, pleading. His playfulness lasted only a few seconds, no more. But it went on, it seemed, and he lived within it, walking up and the down aisle, past the stalls, the white breath of the ponies puffing from their noses.

Afterward, he carried the buns in one arm and with his free hand he broke off a piece and let the ponies lower their heads and take the crumbles, making sure there was enough for all of them. He covered the right stalls and then returned, feeding the ones in the left. At the last stall, Linn pressed his forehead against the pony and shut his eyes, listening to the animal chewing.

"I have to go," he said, his lips grazing the pony's fur. "I have to go now."

He had known this one the longest. He was a pinto and they named him Comet. One evening there had been a meteor shower and Linn and his parents had stayed awake to watch it from the hill, drinking tea with a blanket wrapped around their shoulders. For each star that fell they honored the dead they had known. And the living? Linn had asked, and his father pointed at the ones afloat, not yet dropping, not for years.

The snowfall was heavy now, the sky darkening. In the bathroom Linn opened a cabinet where they kept the bandages. In their new house, wherever it would be, he would do the same, keeping the medicine and the ointments beside the bathtub so that Mihna would know where they were.

The child sat beside the dining room table and he went to her, kneeling to dab ointment on her right cheek. He then unpeeled the bandage and placed it over the cut. "You should be careful," he said, calmly, so that Mihna would know that he was not angry. Her hands were still cold and Linn cupped them and blew his breath onto the tips of his daughter's fingers. "You shouldn't wander alone," he insisted, knowing it was impossible for her to be with him always.

In the past year they had each found their own habits, the patterns that formed their days. He didn't look for her or call for her if she wanted to be alone. He offered her that—her moments of solitude, if she desired it, as he himself did.

How quickly she grew, Linn thought, holding his

daughter's hands, comparing the lengths of their respective fingers, the skin of her palms already turning rough. Happiness with the child had been introducing her to the ponies.

In the kitchen the rice cooker hummed, steam rising from its steel cover. A soup with tofu and vegetables was being heated on the stovetop. On occasion Linn added chili powder, tasting it with a spoon.

"You could start packing, Mihna," he said. Across the room the child sat, swinging her feet like pendulums. Out the front windows, the fields were replaced by his and Mihna's reflections. He opened a newspaper to the apartment listings, skimming the prices. There was still time but now that the farm was no longer his, he felt a sense of urgency. He reminded himself to ask for more boxes at the market. "You'll bring whatever you want," Linn said. "You'll bring the radio."

"Did you give away Mama's dress?" Mihna asked, rubbing the bandage on her face.

It would take time, he knew, for the child. He thought of that. Last night he had dreamed that he was young and his father had come to him from across a field with a pair of horses flanking him. Without speaking, Linn had joined him.

"I kept her clothes," he told Mihna, then returned to the newspaper. There was a house close to the city with a view of the sea. "Would you like the sea?" he asked.

When the soup was heated he ladled it into bowls, Mihna's with rice mixed into it, and brought them to the table. A photograph of Mihna at the base of Tamra Mountain hung on the wall. In the picture she was leaning against the wooden rails that sectioned off the trail. She wore the sunglasses they had bought for her on that day, too large for her head, the plastic frames in the shape of stars.

"She looks pretty in that dress," Mihna said.

He didn't know which dress she was referring to.

"The one in the picture," she said, pointing down the hall, to her bedroom. "The blue one."

Nara had worn it on their honeymoon. He had bought it for her and presented it in a silver box. She had danced in it, at a restaurant, and he followed her lead, not minding the people watching in amusement. He wore a suit. He had never danced before.

"She does look pretty," he said, thinking of her youth. "And I'll give it to you when you're old enough."

He wondered if that would turn out to be true; he hadn't thought of it until now.

"But I don't think she has it," his daughter said.

"Mihna," he said, but the child didn't respond, looking through the window. He finished the soup quickly. He promised he hadn't given it away. He promised one day she would have it. He raised his hand. Mihna, hesitant, took it, this gesture soon transforming into a game of thumb wrestling. The child, smiling now, kneeled atop her chair and leaned forward, her hair skimming her soup. Her thumb moved with vigor and, with her brows furrowed, she slipped her tongue out of her mouth. Her thumb was double-jointed and had the ability to bend backward slightly, a fact Linn used to boast of, for it was said that it predicted the talents of a musician.

When Mihna won, satisfaction rose from the corners of her mouth, her tongue retreating, and she returned to her soup. Linn, standing, wiped the ends of his daughter's hair with a napkin. Mihna ignored him, eating quickly, and Linn told her to slow.

When she was finished, she carried her bowl into the kitchen, where she slid it onto the counter. She returned to the table and took her father's as well and then she retired to her bedroom and listened to the radio. The show she liked wasn't on so she hummed along with the songs, changing into her striped pajamas.

Beside her bed lay the photograph of her mother in the dress. Her mother sat beside a table on a veranda. Her legs were crossed. Something had caught her attention, to her right, and so her face was in profile. Her hair was tucked behind her ears and it hung down over her shoulders. Her mother was twenty-four then, Mihna remembered.

Later, when her father knocked on the door, she hid the photograph under her pillow.

"Mihna," he said, entering. "Is it too cold for you?" He sat beside her, pulling the blanket up to her chin. He was holding a chocolate bar he had half eaten. She had brushed her teeth but he said that he didn't mind, offering the rest. She held it with both of her hands, the pillow tucked under her neck. It was her favorite, he reminded her, picking up the crumbs she dropped while she ate it.

"It'll be a better place," he said, as he had mentioned several times. "A new house. You can help me decide. We'll still see the ponies."

"Papa," she said. "Is there a new house nearby? Are there new neighbors?"

He misunderstood her. He thought she was referring to their departure, that there would be a new house, there would be new neighbors. It would be an adjustment, he said, but he was certain they would be fine. He stroked her hair the way he did with the ponies and he wiped her lips with his thumb and kissed her on the corner of her mouth. His lips felt dry like the grass in the fields during autumn.

It had occurred to her that they were in fact moving so that her father could find another wife, another mother for Mihna. "Divorce," one of the girls at school gossiped, months ago, speaking of someone they knew. It was what they did these days, another girl said. There were the television shows and movies to tell them. "Two husbands," she added. "We will have two. First, for love. Second, for fun."

A box would be packed with her clothes, books, a few dolls, her radio, and the barrettes her mother bought for her. There was going to be a hotel, her father said, and she imagined that once this box was shut, her room would be used for the guests. Her bed would be slept on, her dresser filled. The walls would be repainted, covering the spot beside the closet where she had written her and her parents' name. If someone were to reach up inside the top drawer they would find the chewing gum she placed there. Twelve, she remembered, as hard as stones.

"Papa," she said. "The hotel shouldn't use this bed."

He remained silent and his eyes seemed to tremble slightly but almost at once they returned to their stillness. "We'll take the bed, Mihna," he said, and then said it again.

"And the dresser?"

"It's all yours," he said. "We'll take whatever you want."

When he left, she rose and kneeled on the bed and pressed her nose against the windowpane and tried to picture what, in a few months time, she would see. There wouldn't be ponies and a field, she felt certain, and at night she would no longer see the great dark hands of trees and hear the wind and the cows' singing. All she could see was an emptiness, as though the earth had overturned and all that she remembered lay underground.

She focused on each silhouette rising from the earth. Her eyes lingered on the gate at the field's edge, waiting for it to open. But there was no one.

There was a proper way to care for dresses, Mihna thought, and hoped the woman knew how easily it wrinkled.

She would, aware of this, take it off before bed, changing into a nightgown and brushing her hair with her fingers. The trees would shift closer to give her privacy. The winds would calm. On a branch the dress would hang overnight like a flag waiting to be lowered.

"Goodnight," Mihna said aloud. She lay down and lifted her knees to her chest. Sleep came to her as she imagined her own hair in snow.

The man who had bought the farm returned the following week. As his car climbed the hill, Mihna, who was in the fields, knelt behind Comet and watched his approach from under the pony's belly. The car, however, didn't come to the house. It stopped beside the stable at the bottom of the hill, its engine running. It was late in the morning, bright and sharp, the land like glass. The bordering evergreens were heavy and unmoving. Mihna put on her sunglasses, the frames in the shape of stars, and hummed a song, petting each of the animals.

From the house, her father stepped outside and made his way down to the stable. He waved to her but she did not see him, focused on the man below, who got out of the car and stretched. Soon after, two more people exited, a woman and a girl, perhaps Mihna's age. The closing of the car doors echoed up toward her. They all entered her father's office, the one he used for lessons, and she knew then that they had come to see the ponies. Her father would show them their papers. They would see the photographs on the wall of her riding with her mother.

She did not know where they lived. Perhaps her father would want to be close to them or perhaps the man and his family would move here. A view of the sea, her father had suggested. Higher, up on the floors of a hotel, you would be able to see it, she thought, like blue grass in a meadow. The winds were slow today and they carried with them the smell of seawater and when they paused, she heard the low murmur of waves.

"I'm sorry, Comet," she said, indicating the visitors, and she left him and the others.

It did not take long for her to reach the cliff in the woods. She descended and sat on the boulder, facing the trees and the clearing beyond it. She waited. For how long she wasn't sure but she must have been daydreaming or looking elsewhere for when she blinked, the woman was there, lying in the clearing, in the same position as she was that first time, staring at the sky. She wore the dress that, Mihna was sure now, was her mother's. The neckline was deep and the sash was knotted in the same way her mother tied it, too. She knew there were families of peddlers on the island and backpackers that camped illegally. Perhaps she had lost her way, Mihna considered, and was tired.

This time Mihna did not turn and run. She stepped forward and raised her arm and waved, expecting the woman to turn. "Hi," she called. "You have my mother's dress."

The woman ignored her. Her exhalations hovered above her lips. "Aren't you cold?" Mihna continued, holding her own shoulders, wondering why the woman never turned her head. The longer she stared, the more certain she was that the woman remained perfectly still and she recalled the mannequins in the shop windows when, once a month, her mother took her to the city to shop for clothes. In fact, the only part of the woman that moved, Mihna realized, was her breath, puffing the way she thought a dragon exhaled when it had run out of fire.

"Papa's selling the house," she called. "We'll be leaving. But I'm taking the bed. I'm sorry, but you can't have it."

Mihna stepped closer, walking between the trees. From her pocket she took out the photograph of her mother. "Look," she said. But when she reached the clearing the woman was gone. The winds had stopped; the trees loomed around her. The snow in the clearing was flat and smooth, unbroken by the light of day. She dropped the photograph. The woman had not made a single dent with her body. There were no footprints either.

"Very kind of you to do this," the businessman said, as they walked up the hill to see the ponies. It seemed only fair for his family to try them, the man added, although he knew them to be a first-rate lot. He patted Linn on the shoulder and offered him an envelope filled with money, for the lesson. Linn took it.

His wife was attractive in the way city women were, Linn thought, stylish, with an expensive haircut and smelling of perfume. She wore makeup although he hadn't noticed until he helped her mount Comet, seeing the blush on her cheeks. She was light so that Linn held her with ease and she laughed freely. Her daughter had her mother's face, slender, with fine cheekbones and a high forehead. Her hair was tied back and it swung against the slight wind. She sat atop a dun, much younger than Comet and less prone to mischief.

He had aligned them single file on the field with Comet leading and he stood a few meters away. The riders' hands were close to their waists, the reins held back, and he corrected them, telling them to push their arms forward, to not pull on the reins. They should allow their weight to fall to their heels, he said, and to imagine themselves as puppets, with strings holding aloft their shoulders. Once the ponies were in motion he told them to open their left arm, shifting the rein away from their bodies. On following this command Comet began to circle Linn, the dun close behind. The businessman stood by Linn's side, wiping his forehead with a handkerchief.

All these instructions were a worn language and it came to Linn without thought. The two seemed to be enjoying themselves in their silence, concentrating. The woman led and did not turn around to see how her daughter was faring. How dull for the animals, Linn considered, how patient of them. The sun hung high above the forest and against the snow the ponies' hoofprints lay scattered around him like a hundred planets.

The man had grown distracted. "Back nine," he said,

more to himself, and pointed down below. He walked over to the camphor tree and slapped it, pulling a leaf and crushing it with his fingers to inhale. He dropped the remaining bits onto the ground and then set his legs apart, his shoulders squared, and pivoted his hips, practicing his swing. He whistled as the invisible ball soared above them and Linn, not knowing why, followed its imaginary arc as the ponies circled around him.

When he returned his concentration on the riders, he spotted movement at the edge of the woods. It was Mihna, running out from the trees and then slowing as she entered the fields. Rather than passing through the gate, she sat on the fence and rested her feet on the middle rail. She lowered her elbows on her lap, her face tucked into her open hands.

Linn provided further instruction for the mother and daughter, encouraging them. "Good," he said. "That's good." He did not notice Mihna approach. She startled him, less than a meter away, her footprints trailing her, dark and crooked. Comet, now distracted, broke away from the circle and drew closer to her. She stepped up to the pony and reached for the reins.

"Mihna," he said, going to her quickly and bending down to whisper in her ear. "You shouldn't do that. This is a lesson. You know better." She smelled of snow and her hair was damp. "Go inside now," he said. "You'll catch a cold."

Sitting on Comet, the woman smiled down at the child and greeted her. "Is he yours?" the woman asked.

"Have you been in the forest?" Mihna asked.

"No," the woman said, and held her smile. "Should I?"

"The pony's tired," Mihna said, pulling the reins. Comet whinnied, jerking his head. "He doesn't like strangers. You should go home." She pulled once more and walked away.

Her father called her name. "Come back," he said, angry now, though the child didn't listen. He apologized to the woman.

"Children," she said, laughing, as though about to impart her wisdom. She was interrupted by her husband, who had not witnessed the incident, too intent on his golf swing, but had walked back to them, seeing that his family had paused in their riding. "We'll keep the tree," he said. "Don't you worry about that." He folded his handkerchief and returned it to his jacket pocket.

Linn waited for the man's wife to continue with what she was about to say about children. But she clicked her mouth instead, the way he had been doing, and Comet continued with the lesson.

The next morning Mihna watched as her father unloaded cardboard boxes from the car and carried them into the house. She had gone with him to the market but upon returning home she had rushed to the ponies. The boxes had been flattened, and he tucked a few under his arm so that from this distance they resembled a single brown wing that had sprouted from the side of his body. With his free hand, he opened the door and then went back outside to retrieve more from the trunk of the car.

Mihna left when he was indoors, dragging her toes in the snow. In the woods a bird squawked at her and she looked up and placed her finger to her lips. She pushed her sunglasses up the bridge of her nose and descended the cliff.

The clearing was empty. The photograph of her mother was still there. The woman hadn't come. Or she had but didn't take it. Mihna waited by the boulder. Perhaps she had frightened her. Or perhaps it was the bed the woman wanted all along and she had now gone away, knowing she couldn't have it.

In her hand Mihna clutched a barrette. It had been a gift from her mother for her seventh birthday. Made of small shells, lined along a bridge of steel, her mother had bought it from a sea woman, who sold them on the beach. Carrying it on the flat of her palm, she walked into the clearing and settled it on the snow beside the photograph.

"You can have this if you want," she said, toward the trees. She retreated and waited. When nothing happened, she spoke again. She said, "You can keep it in your hair." She was answered by the winds.

She kneeled beside her unfinished snow house. She resumed building it, using her finger to outline the rooms and the stalls for the ponies. But soon she grew tired of this. She shut her eyes and counted to ten. She lifted her sunglasses and squinted. Her breath paused in the air before parting. In the sky the forest canopy shivered and formed in the shapes of faces, bending toward her. Leaves brushed against each other. "I'm sorry," she called. "You can come back now." She reached down to smooth the footprints she had made and met her shadow.

Linn had hardly said a word to her since the riding lesson. Inside, he waited for his daughter to return. He would ask for her help, he decided. They would make boxes together. He found a roll of clear packing tape in the supply closet— leftover, he realized, from when Nara moved in after their marriage. They hadn't used much of it. She was living closer to the city then, with her own parents. She brought little save for clothes and a box filled with kitchen utensils her mother had given her, her college diploma, and books. Everything else in the house was once his parents' or what he and his wife had accumulated together. He wouldn't keep it all. Some of her clothes he would give away, along with the books they hadn't opened in years. Perhaps, too, some of the furniture, depending on the size of the new house.

Mihna didn't come. At the door he saw that she had left the tree. He called her name, his voice lost in the fields. She was ignoring him, hiding. He grew irritated and went to the living room where he began to assemble the boxes, taping the cardboard bottoms. He worked with speed, the tape making shredding noises whenever he peeled it away from the roll.

He formed a dozen and went about the rooms of the house, dropping a few in each. With a felt-tip pen he marked the tops. He wrote "Mihna" on one of them and placed the box in the corner of her room.

He started with what they had left untouched for months. In the kitchen he wrapped their spare pots and casserole dishes in newspaper. He took down the topmost shelf of books in the living room. In Mihna's room, he packed all the dolls she no longer cared for.

When she eventually returned, she went straight to her bedroom; all at once she rushed out and began to rip the tape off all the boxes in each room. Linn stood in the hallway, silent. She took the books out and then she stood on her toes and attempted to place them onto the top shelf. But she couldn't and so she stacked them against her chest and balanced the pile down the hall and into her bedroom. She shut the door with her foot. Linn followed her. He was about to knock, but stopped. A man's voice erupted from the radio, startling him. It was an advertisement for trips to the mainland. The hotel fare would be included. "Hurry," the man shouted. Then his voice was swallowed by static, the switching of stations, and then silence as Linn pressed his ear against the door and listened to his daughter's calm breathing.

It went on like this. The boxes remained empty, Linn unable to pack. They no longer ate together. He brought her meals and left them in the hallway and only when he was far enough away did she reach for the bowl of soup with a ball of rice placed into the broth. When he asked if she wanted to visit houses for sale, she turned on the radio. He called upon a neighbor to keep Mihna company and he visited the houses alone, some along the beach, ten minutes away from the city, others in the vicinity of the farm.

He spent hours driving, relieved, he admitted, to leave the house. It seemed time had shortened and that Nara had passed away days ago, his daughter once again taciturn, keeping herself in her room. He circled the island, stopping along the coast to watch the surfers in winter. Behind him the tour buses teetered along the winding roads, their windows flashing from the bulbs of cameras. He took off his shoes and felt the snow between his toes. He took in the air of the sea and watched the tides recede.

When he returned, he led the ponies inside before heading to the house, where her bedside lamp cast its light underneath her door. "She hasn't left," the neighbor said. "I'm here," he called after the woman departed, intending to relate to Mihna the places he had visited. He changed his mind and ran water for a bath.

While his daughter slept, he considered the possibility that he did not know her, had never known her, and never would. That his daughter's love for him was love for a dead mother, unearned. He thought of fatherhood and how it seemed he had forgotten what it was, as though he had written its secrets on a sheet of paper that he had misplaced and could not now find. Or perhaps he had been too old when the child came. In his fifties now, he began to believe that their desire to have her was a selfish one. He grew afraid and in fear his weariness expanded, throughout his limbs and into his chest. Some nights he heard her open the door to use the bathroom but he did not rise. He held his breath, waiting for her footsteps to cease, the door to shut, the quiet to return to him.

One late afternoon, however, when he entered the stable, Mihna was there. She was wearing her star-shaped sunglasses. In her arms she carried a large bundle of hay—timothy grass—and she walked down the aisle throwing handfuls of it into the stalls. One of the ponies dragged his portion to a far corner, eating in private. When her arms were emptied of timothy, Linn retrieved another bundle in the empty stall they used for storage. Mihna remained beside Comet, running her fingers through his mane, combing it all to one side.

Linn approached her and, after offering her the hay, he touched her hair, the way she was doing with the pony. She let him. And in this allowance, in touching her, which he had not done, it seemed, in years, he began to cry. He wanted to tell her that when she was older she might understand but he didn't, thinking the words powerless, as he himself felt.

"We have a new neighbor," Mihna said, without looking

at her father, throwing hay into Comet's stall. "She lies in the forest. I used to see her. But she ran away."

Her daughter spoke of a pretty face, a woman's breath the size of a cloud. She lay in the woods, Mihna said, enjoying the whiteness of the ground like an enormous bed. Mihna hadn't recognized her. She asked if it might be someone he knew.

"There's no one, Mihna," he said. "I would know. I would've heard." It was true. The neighbors would have spread such gossip.

"Come see," Mihna kept saying, tugging his sleeve.

"You shouldn't go there," he added. "I've told you. Not by yourself."

"She has the same dress as Mama's. The one in the picture. She doesn't get cold."

"You shouldn't wander alone," her father insisted.

"I like her very much."

"Stop it," her father said.

"Mama gave her the dress."

He grabbed the rest of the hay from her daughter's hands and threw it into Comet's stall. He kneeled in front of her and pulled her sunglasses away, dropping them onto the floor. He gripped her shoulders. "You must understand, Mihna," he said. "You must be patient. You're no longer a child."

Linn didn't realize he was hurting her until he saw her wince and bite her lips. He let go, apologizing, and she held her arms and said, "She doesn't speak."

. . .

That night, as Mihna lay in her bed, Linn searched his bedroom.
He opened the closet, her scent now faded, and pushed aside
each article of clothing on the rack. He moved on to the
dresser, sifting through sweaters, pants, a nightgown Nara
used to wear when she was younger. He looked underneath
the bed, at the boxes they had stored there, taking each one
out and lifting their cardboard tops, removing the sandals and
a bathing suit she wore to the sea. There were gardening gloves
in another box, new and unused, for she bought several pairs
when the store had sales. There were clothes she had saved for
Mihna, when she grew older, jodhpurs, paddock boots, and
T-shirts.

He searched for an hour. He did not find the dress. He
tried to imagine where it could have gone. They had donated
clothes several years ago. Perhaps, by mistake, she had packed
it in there. Or it wasn't a mistake at all. Perhaps it was a dress
she no longer needed and she had asked him first and he had
agreed. Or perhaps he was the one who had gotten rid of it.
He could not recall. It all seemed possible.

He rested on the edge of the bed with his hands on his
lap, staring at his reflection in the dresser mirror: his stooped
posture, his thick gray hair. In this reflection her clothes lay
scattered on the floor and the bed. He saw himself pick them
up, one by one, and begin to refold them, feeling their years
and their seasons, their colors faded, the fabrics worn.

. . .

Mihna, who could not sleep, rose from her bed and pressed her nose against the window. The snow had started again, large flakes of it falling lazily like autumn leaves. She did not know what time it was. The house lay quiet. She exhaled, her breath on the glass expanding. She leaned back and waited for the condensation to recede. When it did so, a silhouette appeared in the distance, under the wide arms of the camphor tree. She blinked. It was still there. It did not appear to move.

Barefoot and in her pajamas, she left her room and walked down the hall, toward her sleeping father. She paused there, the sudden urge to go to him returning, but she remembered his face this afternoon when he had grabbed her shoulders— his frustration, his weary eyes—and she was sorry. It was shame she had felt, but for what she could not articulate. She approached the front entrance of the house and twisted the knob slowly. The door creaked and the winds hurried past her. She listened for her father but he did not wake. She bent down and picked up her boots.

Outside, she let her eyes adjust to the light of the moon. Still warm from her bed, it was not as cold as she expected. The silhouette was still there, motionless. For a short distance, crossing the field, Mihna walked barefoot, enjoying the snow between her toes. When her feet grew cold she paused to put on her boots, all the time keeping her eyes focused on the dark object lest it vanish if she looked away.

It was her father who had told her of spirits and how she could detect them. They were carried by wind. When a car accident occurred, they had, just then, run across the street. When the ponies whinnied one had tickled their noses. In the autumn a leaf fell when they walked under a tree. In the winter they pestered pedestrians by causing them to slip on ice. In the spring they caused people to sneeze. In the summer they broke the electric fans, holding on to the blades. She had once sat in front of one, her hair blowing, waiting for the motor to stop. His stories were endless.

He had never said they were visible, just that they made themselves known by their action, by what they left in their wake.

She was a few meters from the tree when she saw that it wasn't what she expected it to be. It was, rather, Comet, sniffing the snow. He had, as he sometimes did, gotten out of the stable.

Mihna raised her hand to pet the old animal and she watched his breath flame white out of his nostrils. "What are you doing, Comet?" she whispered, and the pony, without provocation, shook his mane and began to trot away. "Comet!" she called to him, as quietly as she could. She clicked her tongue. She whistled softly. He wouldn't listen. She began to follow him, all the while saying his name. The pony trotted across the field. At the gate, he lowered his head and bit down on the latch and lifted. He then pushed the door open with his nose and vanished into the forest.

She began to run. The moonlight faded. She did not think of the dimming of her vision or the branches cutting her skin. She did not think of the woman she had twice seen. She did not think of her mother's death or her own approaching departure as she ran deeper into the woods.

She thought of the pony, the beat of his hooves, his tail fluttering several meters ahead of her. It hung there, suspended, like a wing, and then it rose toward the trees and she chased it and blinked and then it was lost.

The child did not see the trail curve away, and her foot caught the air and she fell. She remained silent and did not cry and in the dark there was a sound like thunder, the snow following.

When Mihna was born, her mother used a blanket as a sling, tied across her body, the knot sticking up over her shoulder like a red flower. In this way she carried the infant in front of her chest. This proved to be useful during feeding, Nara simply lifting up her shirt, Linn looking away. She would tease him about this, his avoidance, what he thought of as courtesy and what she thought of as distance. "You've seen it before, Linn," she teased him, as the warm gums of her daughter clung to her.

There were also the days when she turned the sling around so that the child hung across her back, the blanket used as a seat. Mihna would hold her mother at the base of her neck and she fell asleep with the lulling rhythm of Nara's gait as they traversed the fields. This was spring. And Nara, her body no longer a host, woke every morning with an abundance of energy, her voice loud and confident, her eyes sharp. At night, in bed, she would run her hands along Linn's stomach, as if a part of her had to be in motion always, even in sleep. She cooked furiously and started a garden behind the house, Mihna either on her back or in front of her chest.

And it was with her child in the sling that she sat under the camphor tree in the afternoons. She would reach up to break off a leaf and crush it with her fingers, its scent hovering about them as she followed the curve of the hills, the sky dropping behind the ridges. To Mihna she sang folksongs she remembered when she herself was young. "Look for me in the camphor tree," she hummed, "wait for me under forsythia, be with me beside camellia." And to this melody the child slept in the shadows of the broad leaves, her ear pressed against her mother's breasts, listening to the song reverberate from within.

"Look for me in the camphor tree," she used to say to Linn, heading outside for the day, carrying Mihna. "Look for us there." It had been in jest. But after the lessons or cleaning the stable he looked each time, up into the tree, covering his eyes from the sun, wondering if the branch swaying was his wife's leg or whether a certain leaf was in the shape of his daughter's head.

They had been happy then, though thinking of it now, it

was her happiness first and not his, one that she had offered to him and one that he received. It was her time, hers alone, always, with the child, and he, later on, the visitor.

He recalled all this when he woke, and for an instant he did not know where he was. Light played along the ceiling, the shadows of branches from the backyard like waving hands. He was convinced he was outdoors, that he had somehow slept out there, but his vision focused and he rose from the bed, the room returned. A thought occurred to him then: perhaps it had been in haste. Perhaps they could stay. The years would unfold of their own accord. But such thoughts were short-lived as he heard the telephone ring, then a message. It was the hotel owner, who spoke of bringing contractors to the grounds next week. Linn entered the hallway. At Mihna's door he heard the silence of sleep.

After dressing and pouring hot coffee into a thermos, he crossed the fields, as he had done all his life, his father before that, and went to the stable. At its entrance he saw the door open and Comet's stall empty. He shook his head, in part due to amusement, in part due to annoyance. He set the thermos down against the wall and turned to look out across the fields.

The snow from yesterday had stopped, though whatever tracks they once showed were now filled. He saw his own footprints, nothing more. The sun shone with warmth and he shut his eyes as it washed his neck and he felt it slipping down his shirt and across his chest. He yawned, not yet having had the coffee, and set out toward the hills.

It did not take long for him to find Comet in the forest, lying down at the bottom of a small cliff, the pinto pattern brilliant against the trees. Linn whistled but was ignored, so he went to the animal, bending branches.

The pony had stumbled upon a clearing and was whinnying softly. He lay with his belly against the snow and his front legs tucked underneath him. He was holding something against his shoulder, his neck wrapped around it and craned toward his belly. But it wasn't until Linn stepped closer that he saw it was Mihna lying curled against him. She lay with one knee raised, dressed in her striped pajamas, torn at the knees, her feet covered in a pair of untied boots. Snow clung to her hair and her body as if it had grown out of her. On occasion the animal shifted his legs and licked her, melting the snow. She lay looking down at a photograph of Nara, wiping away the pony's breath from it. A barrette lay beside her hip. Nearby there was an unfinished house made of snow, the child's gloved fingers imprinted onto its walls. Whether she noticed Linn he could not tell.

He did not to go to her immediately. He stood there at the edge of the clearing, uncertain of whether to go any farther. This land he knew. He had lived here all his life. He had never left. Yet it seemed to him then that he had arrived in a foreign land, in some forgotten country where an entire people had already gone, what remained left for the seasons. He neither recognized the clearing nor the trees.

He had seen his father once, bathing outdoors in the summer, reaching down for the bucket, his back stooped to reveal the wound of a bullet Linn had never known existed. He was, perhaps, Mihna's age, and he quickly hid behind the window, convinced in that moment that the bullet was still inside the man, tied by an invisible string that could pull his father back into a world Linn could not imagine in its vastness. It was not a time his father spoke of often, a time when he was away and his own wife waited. He had come out of the woods, Linn's mother had said. When the war finished. He had come by horse.

When Linn eventually stepped into the clearing, the pony moved away and he lifted his daughter, who placed her arms around his neck, resting her head on his shoulder. She had winced and he asked her if she were hurt. He said her name. She did not respond, her eyes closed, her body going limp. She smelled of the woods. He smoothed her hair. The pony, who had begun to climb the trail, assuming they would follow, stopped to look back at them.

"We are going," Linn kept repeating. "We are going now." But the conviction of these words had already left him. So he stood there, in the middle of that clearing, rocking her, as his wife used to, and it was then his daughter opened her eyes, raised her head, and brushed his ear with her lips. And then she spoke. About nighttime and its noises. About castles and corridors. About foxes and maidens. About a woman in a pale blue dress. All the while he held her. Her warm breath against him, her faint voice in that cold light. Snow began to fall. He looked up. The evergreens swayed, slow moving in the air and wide as ships.

AND WE WILL BE HERE

EACH DAY SHE WOKE BEFORE DAWN and walked the grounds of the American hospital. She didn't go far. She kept to the footpaths that encircled the main hall, past the evergreens and the timber cottages now used as additional wards for the wounded.

It had once been a Japanese vocational school for the arts and she remembered the painter who had asked her and Junpei to model. They had been walking past the school that afternoon and the young man had called to them. He led them under the gate and to a tree, where she sat with Junpei between her legs. She pretended to read to her companion, though it wasn't a book she held. The painter had instead given her his hat and told her to imagine. It was made of wool and smelled of sweat and pine and the band inside had worn away so that strands of it fell onto her wrist. She had never been inside the school until then, though she passed it often and would later wonder behind which window the painter lived. The shadows of leaves moved across their arms. They kept still. Beside them was a stone garden. She never saw the young man again.

Her name was Miya and twenty-five years had passed since that day, though lately she found herself thinking about the painter as she took her walks around the hospital. Or not him exactly, but the painting, which she never saw finished. Perhaps it had hung someplace in the school's corridors. Or in someone's home or even at a museum, she thought, when she was feeling fanciful. Perhaps he had become famous and she was unaware of it. She wondered how many people had seen their image there, under that tree, and how many questioned who the children were, if they did at all.

She did not own any childhood photographs of herself and did not have anyone to tell her what she looked like then. She believed she was now thirty-four years old but wasn't certain. There wasn't anyone to tell her about that, either. She had been born in Japan, she knew, and had come to Korea at an early age, to this island south of the peninsula. But she had no memory of this journey or any time before that. Hers was a life adapted, she would have said, if someone asked.

The woman who raised her had passed away from sickness. Miya had brought her to the hospital and she remembered this as well, their kindness, Miss Hara among the soldiers. They had liked Miss Hara and a group of doctors once sang for her while she was dying. It was an American song. Barbershop, someone said, and she didn't know what that meant. Miss Hara smiled at them and gripped the footboard with her toes. This was two years ago.

She didn't know then that she would leave the orphanage and return to this place, assisting the nurses with the wounded. A volunteer, the doctor named Henry suggested, and she thought it a fine word. He was tall with freckled skin and a broad forehead. "Help is always needed," he said, and escorted her inside. On that first day he gave her a hospital gown and she was puzzled. He shrugged, embarrassed. They were low on supplies. The gowns were comfortable, he said, and even provided her with a nurse's cap so everyone could tell her apart from the others.

Every day she brought the soldiers water. She trimmed their hair if it tickled their ears. She scratched their backs. She made them fresh lemonade from the citrus grove. She spoke to them if conversation was what they desired. She wheeled them out of the wards for a bit of air. She worked until her body grew numb. A thousand beds and convalescents scattered throughout the buildings.

"What's your name?" she always asked. "Where are you from?" Australia, someone said. Another: Greece. She had met men from France, New Zealand, Thailand, America, and the peninsula. With every new arrival she searched their faces, pushing the gurney or the wheelchair through the corridors. A man's nose reminded her of someone she once knew. Someone else's lips curved downward the way hers did. She found the eyes of Miss Hara. Junpei's chin. The familiar touch of skin. A scar on the elbow.

I knew you once, she would think, moving through the wards as if she had done so all her life.

Her own room was on the second floor of the main hall, and when she wasn't occupied with a patient or when Henry told her to rest, she retired there. It wasn't much: a single bed, a desk beside a window. The walls were bare. She owned few possessions. She had a teacup, a comb, an extra set of clothes, and a sewing machine, all taken from the orphanage.

She sewed old gowns and soldiers' uniforms if they could be saved. She sipped water from the teacup for she wasn't sure if she could ask for tea. She kept the door closed. A bare light bulb hung from the ceiling, casting a dome around her. Finished with her clothes, she would push the sewing machine aside and study the surface of the desk, where someone had painted what she assumed were landmasses, the texture of it thick and rising in places. Who did it or how long it had been there she didn't know. With her finger she traced the outlines of her imagined nations until sleep came to her and she lay on her bed and shut her eyes and felt the satisfaction of a day fulfilled.

These were her days. In their patterns she found comfort. Not once in two years had she left the hospital property. Instead, she kept watch over the grounds, pacing within its border and following the footpaths every morning before dawn.

On some days she climbed the tree beside the stone garden. From this distance she could see the campus in its intended symmetry. The main hall at the center, its roof of red tiles, weather-worn, and the eaves that shaded the stucco walls. The courtyard and the cottages. The citrus grove and the hills beyond which lay the orphanage. A horizon formed by coastal mountains, their peaks covered in the remnants of last month's snow. The color of the land muted.

None of it had changed, she thought. Any moment now the students would appear from the main hall, as they used to, she herself standing on the other side of the fence. She imagined this, repeating it in her mind, and waited for the sun to rise, her arms hooked around a branch, her legs dangling, the world, it seemed, not yet awake. The war was far.

And it was here one morning, up in the tree, that she witnessed the cargo trucks coming down the main road. She had grown accustomed to them, of course, but with every visit she felt her heart quicken. Headlights crowned the hill. There was the low pitch of a radio. She heard a woman's voice, singing, accompanied by a brass band that seemed to float across the fields, caught by the winds. The trucks grew closer, rumbling. In their approach they resembled elephants. Dust sprayed underneath their wheels. They turned into the driveway and parked in the courtyard, their engines idle, their headlights sweeping across the field.

All at once men tumbled out of the cargo holds, their

bodies shadowed against the low sky. Scurrying like thieves. Some knelt on the grass and appeared to be digging. Then the air popped and the grass caught fire, first in one corner, then in another, and another, as if the ground had cracked open to illuminate the stretchers, dozens of them, already spread out on the lawn.

Miya climbed down the tree and brushed away dirt from her hospital gown. She tucked the loose strands of her hair behind her ears and put on her nurse's cap. She followed the path to the driveway, engulfed by the smoke of flares and the scent of the wounded. She helped a nurse lift a stretcher, shocked by the soldier's lightness. He was an American. His gaze lolled and his breath was sour. The nurse led them past the doors and into the main hall.

"What's your name?" Miya asked the soldier. "Where are you from?"

He looked up at her, seeing her upside down. He grinned. "Hi, doll face," he said. "I'm Benson from Boston."

"Hello, Benson from Boston," she said, and the American blinked and his smile vanished. When he was settled into a bed she took his hand.

Soon after, a patient was placed on the bed beside Benson's. She didn't go to him until later, curious, parting the curtain to reveal a young man with gauze wrapped around his head and bandages over his eyes. He was a mainlander, perhaps. Or an island native. He was comatose, she realized, and asked Benson whether he knew who the patient was. Benson didn't respond, staring up at the ceiling as he would for most of his time here. She checked to see if Henry was close by. He was at the end of the ward. She turned again toward the bandaged patient and shut the curtain behind her.

She leaned forward. It was as though layers of his body had been stripped. "Hello," she whispered, not yet recognizing him. The sun had risen and the ward blazed white for a moment before the clouds passed. She lifted the bandages away from his eyes, then quickly drew her hand back as if stung. She looked around, disoriented, clutching the bed sheet. *She knew him,* she kept repeating, though no one responded. *She knew him.* He was there, within this face, this aged body, she was certain of it. But her voice had failed her and so she spoke in silence about how long it had been and how he had come back, as she knew he would, this boy, whom she held under a tree, many years ago, while a man painted their likeness.

She was woken by the fading thunder of aircraft. Then the quiet returned and she lay listening to the sound of breathing. She was unsure of the time. Her eyes adjusted to the faint light from the windows, the convalescents lined up along the walls like dark monuments. She had fallen asleep on a chair beside Junpei's bed.

Benson was muttering, "I didn't do nothing. I didn't do nothing at all." She crossed over to him and massaged his temples with her fingertips. He was sweating. A fever. She went to the sink and soaked a cloth in cold water and then draped it over Benson's forehead. A nurse passed her, yawning. "Get some sleep, Miya," she whispered, heading to the quarters. Miya put on her coat. And then, looking back at Junpei, his shadowed body under a sheet, she stepped outside, breathing in the air.

At the stone garden she sat on the bench and took off her shoes. The garden's terrain was made of sand, raked to resemble currents of water running beside the stones. She placed her feet into the sand and felt the coolness of it and then the quick warmth, as though the earth were a hand tugging at her ankles. She looked up at the tree and then drifted into sleep once more, facing the dark windows of the ward.

In daylight she rose to the footsteps of convalescents and nurses. At the grove she plucked a lemon, slipping it into her pocket before returning inside. Junpei lay with his arms to his side. She leaned forward and inhaled his raspy breath and saw the child she remembered still there along the bottom half of his face. She brought the lemon to her mouth and bit into the rind, breaking away the flesh. She squeezed the juice onto a wet cloth and began to clean his chin, wiping away dirt and crusted blood.

"You'll need a proper bath, soon," she said. "Like everyone else here. It's no longer a school, you know. But there is still the tree. And the stone garden. Of course there is."

They found him beside the remnants of a house, she was told. "He wouldn't have gone inside first," Henry said, examining the patient's legs. "We'd have nothing left of him if he did."

She ran her fingers over his bandages, guessing where his eyebrows were hidden. "Where have you been, Junpei?" she asked him, cleaning his hands.

She had witnessed his first step, she recalled. At the orphanage's entrance. Once learned, he walked all throughout the day, the child's face filled with determination as he swayed his hips and his arms, shuffling past the dormitory, the classrooms, the barn—out toward the fences as well, ignoring Miya's pleas for him to slow. When she was doing her chores he would walk back and forth beside her, in circles, some form of fury in him, his body unwilling to pause until they were called for supper, where he would sit on her lap, his head bowed, as if catching up on a day's worth of breathing. "Messenger," the children called him.

· The orphanage was still there, she knew, on the other side of the western hills. It had expanded over the years, housing children from the war. She did not go to it anymore.

She and Junpei had arrived at the same time. An earthquake had destroyed Tokyo. They had, along with hundreds of others, been airlifted to this island, which was under Japanese rule then. Solla, it was called. Their ages were guessed. Names were given. They had not known each other before. They were paired together and slept on a blanket on the floor, her arm tucked under his head. They lay on their sides, facing each other, their bodies in the shape of prayer. Junpei's hair caught in her teeth when she woke in the mornings.

In those early years she bathed him. She filled unused fuel barrels with water and lifted the boy into it. He would cling to her ears as she washed his chest. When he was older, she brought Junpei to Miss Hara's lessons, learning both Japanese and Korean to communicate with the local islanders. They were taught songs, mathematics as well. They helped with the house chores, wiping windows with newspaper, mopping the floors, taking breaks to duel with brooms in the yard. They took walks through the forest and up the hills to view the ocean. They walked to the school, counting all the artists they could see behind windows. Not once did they speak of Tokyo.

When the boy was nearly Miya's height, Miss Hara asked him whether he now preferred to stay with the other boys. He shook his head, clutching Miya's hand, and she felt the surety of his grip and was convinced in that moment that they would grow old together—that theirs was a shared life. She would, at night, tell him of this. A house by the sea. They would fish. They would plant a garden. "Horses," she would add, facing him, her fingers galloping across his shoulders lit by the moon.

She would always remember that morning when he left her in the yard to chase a crow. In memory there was his face and only that, the open mouth, his wet eyes, his return, his hands picking at his clothes, an animal-like cry erupting from the center of his body. How he held her and she, unable to calm him, saw Miss Hara hurrying to the barn. Miya followed. A crowd had formed. They were all gazing up.

It took her a moment to realize that what hung from the rafters was in fact a person and not a doll, his limbs dangling, as if filled with cotton. It was a boy, his face discolored from the rope around his neck. And there was Junpei behind her, clutching her waist, pointing at the floor where a shoe had fallen. No one else noticed.

After this, Junpei began to wander. She would wake to find that he had already risen. Or she would be washing clothes and turn to see that he had disappeared. He missed his lessons. In the evenings he didn't show up for supper. She searched the dormitory and the classrooms. She searched the barn and the fields. She ran down the road and saw at last his figure in the distance, standing there by the fence, his hands rooted into his pockets.

"Junpei," she called one evening, taking hold of his wrist. "Where have you been?"

It was growing dark. He wouldn't look at her, his eyes roaming over the mountains. "Not far," he said.

"Miss Hara will be worried," she said, tugging on his arm. "Come."

She turned and he followed her. At the orphanage they slept as they always did, facing each other. Sometime later he woke her with his voice. "I can't find it, Miya. I've looked everywhere. For the other one. He was barefoot, you know. I saw his toes." He drifted, the words slipping, and she dreamed of a boy who would not stop walking.

In six month's time, Junpei was gone. They had been at the orphanage for over a decade. It was the beginning of winter. Snow had yet to fall. She went to bathe. Upon her return, he wasn't there. The schoolbag they shared was missing, their pillow as well. Miya, wearing her nightgown, rushed to the road and called his name and waited. Her hair began to freeze. Miss Hara found her that afternoon, still waiting. With her hands she had torn the hem of her gown.

It was the year an American woman named Earhart had flown over the Pacific. From Hawaii to California. She recalled that she and Junpei had heard through the radio. That evening they climbed the hill behind the orphanage. They walked to the edge of the cliff. They raised their hands above their eyes and peered out at the horizon until the ocean faded.

All that week she remained beside him, vigilant. Benson ignored her, staring up at the ceiling. With her head resting on her hand she watched Junpei. The flat bridge of his nose. The curve of his cheekbones. His chapped lips. She dipped her finger in lemon water and placed it into his mouth, convinced that in his sleep it would sink into the soil of his tongue and he would dream of citrus. She felt his teeth, like crags, the one he had lost a mystery to her, this empty space near the front, an incomplete thought. The hair on his face was beginning to grow. He smelled of staleness and storage. She pressed her thumbs against the calloused skin of his feet, feeling for any traces of where he had been.

She spoke to him. Of her years. Of what he had missed. "You still have your youth," she told him. "You'll get used to things here."

She attempted to imagine his own years away but couldn't. They were an undecipherable map, with nameless cities and towns, borderless countries. She saw him forever on a boat following the routes along the Pacific, absent of history, invisible to it. He would have woken one day in a cabin, feeling the ocean shudder, great spires of smoke in the far distance in Japan, as if the entire country were evaporating. He would not have thought of her then.

And would he have ever gone to Tokyo? She wasn't sure. She didn't think so. She never believed he had gone in search of that. Instead, he had fled. Sure of this, she fell asleep beside him, speaking of gardens to his silent face.

She was startled from a dream she couldn't remember. Carrying a lamp she wandered the hospital's corridors, as she did when she first arrived. In the hallways she brought the light up to the walls, pushing away the moonlight. On first glance the walls were bare, nondescript, the paint yellowed by age and dust. The longer she stared, however, bright rectangular shapes rose out of them, spaced out evenly along the walls like ghost windows.

She had searched for paintings before. She used to ask Henry about them but he shrugged, indifferent. All that night she looked again. First she explored the main hall, taking the staircase quietly. There were so many doors. She paused at each of them, listening to a patient's breathing. If she heard nothing, she slid the doors open and inspected the rooms now used to store equipment, cans of food, extra mattresses. She went outside and into the cottages, opening closets, waking the patients there. They looked at her perplexed, and she brought a finger to her lips as if sharing some kind of secret. She hunted with all that was left of her energy, releasing it in a great burst.

Exhausted, she headed to the stone garden. The moon hung over the crest of the hills, an even light spreading over the grass, the tree, and the sand that sparkled like diamonds. Midway there she stopped. One of the stones had moved. She squinted, then rubbed her eyes with her palms, shaking her head, feeling her limbs grow heavy. The stone moved again. It rose. It began to approach her and she clenched her fists, wondering to what world she had entered in these hours. Closer, it grew skin and then a face formed and she saw that it was a boy, no older than thirteen.

"Hey, Miss," the boy said, in the island dialect. "I hear your footsteps. All over." He tapped his earlobes. He was dressed in dark pants, a button-down shirt and rubber moccasins. His head was shaved and he had thin lips. A small leather pouch hung from his belt loop. He asked what Miya was looking for.

"Paintings," Miya replied. "Seen any?"

Laughter erupted from the boy's small mouth. "I see nothing," he said, and motioned for her to step closer.

She did so, bending forward. The boy's eyes were fogged, like porcelain. He reached up to touch Miya's face, extending his fingers along her jawline and then closing them over her nose. His palms smelled of cinnamon. He wrapped a hand around her pinky finger. "Come with me," he said, leading her to the stone garden.

Was he a patient? she asked. Another volunteer?

He didn't respond. He sat on the garden's edge and began to wipe the waves away in the sand until the surface was smooth. He opened his pouch and dug his fingers into it, lifting his hand to reveal dozens of marbles. These he placed in the middle of the sandbox, adjusting the cluster, each orb illuminating colors under the night sky. Satisfied, he offered another marble to Miya. She took it and lay on her stomach in the grass. She aimed. She flicked her thumb and followed the marble's path over the surface of the sand as it ricocheted against the others. The boy lay down beside her. His hands rested on his chin, his legs swinging in the air.

"What does it look like?" the boy asked.

She turned onto her back. Stars formed into shapes and

then broke apart. The blinking dot of an airplane moved from left to right, vanishing behind the silhouettes of branches. She used to wait for Junpei to return. She would climb trees at the orphanage, the ground below shrinking. The forest canopy opened to her like the waves of the sea and a flock of birds rose out of it, spraying leaves. She waited for boats.

The boy nudged her, breathing into her ear, pointing at the marbles. "Hey, Miss," he said, repeating his question.

"Fireworks," Miya responded.

The following morning the boy was gone. The day was warmer than the others. The sun had settled onto her skin. The ground was damp. When she rose from the garden she saw the land had created a cast of her body: grass folded pale to form her slightly parted legs, the curve of her shoulders, the sand indented where she had rested her head. Beside that was the shape of the boy, too, though it appeared he had been lying on his side, watching her. Or was it that? Her certainty, an instant before so sure, abandoned her. A wind came and stole the shapes. She looked for the marbles' paths but they had been erased as well, replaced by the waves that were always there. The rake lay under the bench like an old rifle. She brushed sand from her hair.

Inside, she found Henry tending to a soldier who was recovering from surgery. They were sending him to a rehabilitation clinic in Virginia, Henry told him. The soldier seemed pleased with the news. They shook hands. The doctor continued with his rounds. She stood in the ward's entrance for a moment and watched the soldier sit up in bed suddenly, stretch forward, fingers extended, and touch the space where his legs had once been.

She approached Junpei's bed. If she stared at him long enough it seemed he wasn't breathing. Or as if the entire room was, rising and falling. Henry was beside her now, making note of Junpei's vitals. He was holding the nurse's cap he had given to her. She must have dropped it somewhere.

"Junpei you said his name was?" Henry asked, without looking at the chart.

"There was a boy," Miya said. "He is blind. A native. Have you seen him?"

Henry kept his gaze on her and shook his head.

"Is he a volunteer?" she asked.

"Miya."

"He wore dark pants and moccasins. Perhaps he was a patient."

Henry looked over her shoulder and she saw the tiredness of his skin. He took her arm and led her outside to the corridor. They stood by a window and his brown hair speckled in sunlight.

"He carries marbles. In a little pouch."

"Miya," Henry repeated. "You aren't sleeping." He spoke in a whisper. "We've talked about this. Do you remember? You're of no use to me if you aren't sleeping."

She took her cap and put it on.

"There are others you could tend to," he continued.

She ignored him. She had known Henry for two years now. He had been one of the singers when the orphanage director was here. She avoided his stare and returned to Junpei and his stillness. She placed lemon juice onto his lips and then combed his hair with her fingers. She had done the same for Miss Hara and spent the days reading to her from a book of folktales, keeping her company as the woman drifted in and out of consciousness.

"Has he been bathed?" she asked Henry. "It's time, I think. Don't you agree? We could remove the bandages, also. From his eyes. It can't be good for him. He would wake to see nothing."

In Henry's hand was a tin cup filled with two tablets. "For your headache, Miya," he said.

Had she complained of that? She couldn't recall. She took the pills, slipping them under her tongue.

"Rest for an hour," he encouraged her. "You need your strength. Do you remember, Miya? Like we said. You need to rest."

He took her arm again and led her upstairs to her room. She didn't protest. After he left she spat out the pills and ground them on the floor with the bottom of her teacup. She then gathered the powder into her hand and blew it out the window, watching it scatter.

She turned to her sewing machine. At the base, written in English were the words: *Little Betty.* "Hello, Betty," she said. "Where are you from?" From a basket on the floor she picked up a torn shirt and placed it on the tray. She couldn't recall to whom it belonged. She cranked the wheel and the spool on top rotated, unwinding the gray thread. The machine was rusting. The paint on the desk formed continents.

Through the walls she heard a man's voice on the radio. It was the news. There was to be a UN prisoner exchange with the North and the Chinese. Hill 255 was in the shape of a pork chop, another news segment explained. She wondered who had thought of that first, who called these things such names. Her window faced the front courtyard and beyond that were the main road and the hills that led to the orphanage. The hills were in the shape of ears, she thought, the sides of heads. Below her the main entrance opened and a soldier, discharged, stepped out onto the patio in uniform. He raised his hand to shade his eyes and looked around him as if he weren't sure where he was and how he had come here.

After Junpei left the orphanage, Miya turned silent. She performed her chores with a mechanical precision and then did more, relieving the other children of their responsibilities. They avoided her, unsure of what to say. She didn't notice. The weeks passed and she slept little, wandering the grounds and out to the field's edge where the forest began.

She was chopping wood behind the kitchen one afternoon when Miss Hara approached her. Together, without speaking, they carried the split logs to the furnaces. She had cut extra and brought them to Miss Hara's cottage, where she placed them at the doorstep. Miss Hara invited her inside. She was a slim woman with a receding hairline. She had long slender fingers that wrapped around her arms as she gazed down at Miya.

She had never seen the inside of the house before. It was sparse in its furnishings. A single tea table, a low desk beside the window where the woman kneeled and wrote letters. The walls were unadorned.

Miss Hara owned a single teacup and that evening they drank tea sitting on the floor, passing the cup back and forth as they watched the fire. Miya expected the woman would mention Junpei in some way but she didn't. She stood to retrieve a sheet of paper and a pencil. "Much to do," she said, and sighed. She told Miya of her plans for the next day. A list was drawn. She handed Miya the list and, smiling, lifted her hand and waved her off.

The next day Miya assigned chores to the younger ones: who would be picking vegetables in the garden, milking the cows, cooking, washing linen, cleaning the hallways and the dormitory. She made sure the mats were rolled and the floors swept. She enforced curfew. She led the children to the stable and fed the ponies, bringing their manure out to the field where she spread it over the soil.

She returned to Miss Hara, handing her the list. Miss Hara gave her another one. Again, she drank tea with the woman in silence. Another day came. Another list was given. In the years to come, she would, along with the others her age, begin to tutor the children.

She stayed, as did many. When a new child arrived, she was the first to carry them or take their hand, escorting them into the kitchen. The hours were quick and arduous. In her time, some, like Junpei, ran away, though this was rare. Even so, she grew used to this. And for those who approached her about leaving, Miya and Miss Hara assisted them in obtaining work with the local farmers and the fishermen. They would all gather in front of the orphanage and watch each child depart on a pony, their new employer guiding them down the road. There was even a marriage. They held a wedding ceremony. As a wedding gift the orphans built a house at the end of the field.

All the days ended at Miss Hara's cottage and a single cup of tea. Few words were spoken. Lists were no longer required. Some nights they ignored each other completely, Miss Hara writing her letters, Miya reading a book. At exactly the same hour each day Miss Hara would turn to her and wave her away by flicking her hand. "Good night, Miss Hara," Miya said, and the woman nodded, smiling.

It was in the summer, in the evening, that she saw the flicker of a lamp at the end of the road. A birthday had been celebrated, marking the day she arrived. She was, by Miss

Hara's calculation, twenty-six. Japan was at war. Some of the island's residents had been enlisted to fight alongside them. She sat on the floor, gripping the windowsill, watching the light sway and grow larger. It beat in the rhythm of her heart. Then she saw the figure that held it. She rushed outside.

"Junpei!" she called, running toward him. "Junpei!"

The young man paused, perplexed, and looked at her, raising the lamp to Miya's face. "Aren't you pretty," he said, and drank from a bottle of wine. He stepped closer. He ran his fingers down the length of her hair. She didn't move away. He was sweating. He spat. "You are not from here," he said. He then grasped her hand and lowered it between his legs and she felt him and stood there, studying the shape of his body.

The broom appeared like a spear thrown across Miya's shoulder. She turned and there was the shadow of Miss Hara in the dark, raising her arms and beating the man. He had dropped the bottle and Miss Hara took it, shattered it on the ground, and stabbed the air with the broken bottleneck. She did this until the man was down the road and when he was gone she turned to Miya, who had begun to cry, and slapped her across the face and continued to do so until Miya fell. Miss Hara left her there.

In the middle of the night, after Miya had returned to the dormitory, Miss Hara came to her and took her back to the house. The woman washed the girl's face. They shared the mat, lying beside each other and looking up at the beams along the ceiling and the starlight that swept over them.

In the first week of August the bombs fell on Hiroshima and Nagasaki. And all the orphans woke one day to find that the Japanese army had left. The Americans came in their place. Cargo trucks could be seen on the roads and Miya kept waiting for the soldiers to take her and the others away. Instead, supplies were offered to them, including clothing, coffee, sugar, and toys. "Islanders," they were called, with affection, and she realized she had been here for over twenty years.

So the orphanage remained. The school across the hills, however, was abandoned. She no longer walked to it. At night she heard the distant engines of trucks and imagined the students leaving and the Americans carrying crates of artwork out of the buildings, sending them off on ships across the Pacific.

Miss Hara had begun to teach her how to sew, from a machine they were given by an American chaplain. They sat beside her desk and Miya pushed the fabric under the machine's needle while Miss Hara turned the wheel. A lamp was burning and the shadows of their arms loomed across the floor like birds. By then another war had started, this time on the peninsula.

All of a sudden Miss Hara spoke. "I have my vocation," she said, guiding Miya's fingers. "What will yours be?"

Miya didn't respond. She had never heard Miss Hara speak so many words outside of the classroom. The tapping noise of the sewing machine filled the room, as well as the woman's quick breathing. Her voice remained calm.

"I'm not the judge of this. But there is a world outside of this one. And someday they will go home. And we will be here."

She left to check on their tea. Miya spun the wheel herself. She heard the cup drop and looked back to see Miss Hara's outstretched arm on the floor behind a counter, the cup swiveling rapidly, then slowing. The sewing machine needle punched into Miya's finger.

She would, at times, attempt to recall those hours. It would only come to her in quick images. Her attempts at waking the woman. Running to the barn for a pony. Her own rapid breathing, the tremor of her heart. Her desire to shout, yet inability to. Her inexplicable strength in lifting the body onto the pony's back. Her galloping. Her ascent up the hills and crossing over them. Dusk.

For the second time in her life, she passed through the gates of the school. A young nurse, upon hearing the sound of hooves, stepped out onto the patio. Behind her, the faces of convalescents began to fill the windows, their eyes betraying curiosity and bewilderment, this girl on a pony, a woman's body slumped forward against the animal's neck.

The young doctor she would later come to know as Henry stepped forward, carrying a stretcher. Miss Hara was brought inside and placed on a bed. He thought at first the woman had been wounded. Blood streaked her face and clothes. Henry searched for the source. He couldn't find it. He turned to Miya and then saw her finger.

She returned to the orphanage after Miss Hara passed away. An American organization had decided to take over the institution. A married couple moved into Miss Hara's cottage. The husband translated. They were from the Midwest, they told Miya, and she didn't know what state that was. Each night they read the Bible before supper. They taught the children English and refused to allow the girls to bathe with the boys. Chaplains visited. Journalists, also. The dormitory filled with orphans from the mainland cities and towns.

Miya lasted there two months. The others stood in front of the orphanage to bid her farewell. She gathered Miss Hara's teacup, an extra set of clothes, a comb, her unsent letters, which Miya had hidden, and placed them all into a satchel. She carried this and the sewing machine to the car that was to take her back to the hospital.

Later, in the room Henry offered her, she would read over Miss Hara's letters. Most were requesting supplies, from the UN and Christian communities. The last stack, however, was a list: in columns were the names of orphans, copied onto dozens of sheets of paper in the woman's handwriting, all addressed to refugee camps in the mainland and towns in Japan. *Found*, it stated, at the top.

She looked for herself. She wasn't there, of course. She was nameless when she arrived, her age estimated. As was Junpei. She was about to put the letter away but then paused at the last person on the list. It was written as if it had been an afterthought, the handwriting less confident. She hadn't known Miss Hara's full name until then.

In the washroom she filled her teacup with water and then added salt taken from the kitchen. It was night, the room windowless. A light bulb hung from the ceiling, giving off a dull glow. She covered the cup with her hand and shook the liquid mixture. She then rubbed the saltwater onto her teeth and along the base of her gums. What remained in the cup she swirled in her mouth and then returned to her room. She didn't bother with the light. Outside the hills faded into sky. She was wearing her hospital gown. She sat on the edge of the bed and combed her hair. The shirt she had sewn lay folded on her desk. Barefoot, she walked downstairs and into the ward.

Two nurses were making their rounds. They nodded to her and she returned their greeting. A weak light shone through the windows, touching the shoulders of the wounded. Someone coughed. Bed sheets rustled. There was the scent of ether and iodine. She passed the curtain, leaving it parted, and stood above Junpei. She leaned over him, toward the window, and peered out at the tree and the stone garden. A bird lifted off a branch, a speck of shadow. She watched the stones for movement. "Where are you?" she said.

"Where is who?"

She looked down at Junpei. His face was motionless, his

eyes still covered. She leaned down and placed her ear against his dry lips.

In the next bed over Benson lifted his arms. He was lying on his back, staring up at the ceiling. His chest was wrapped in gauze. "Where is who?" he repeated.

"Hello, Benson," she said, and asked if she could get him anything. He didn't respond.

She crossed the room to the sink and filled a bowl with warm water. She pumped powdered soap into it from the dispenser and then placed it beside Junpei's bed. "You stink," she said, laughing quietly, and patted Junpei's hand. "You've been neglected, you poor thing."

"What did you dream last night?" Benson called.

She didn't know. She unbuttoned Junpei's shirt and spread it out over the ends of the bed. There were bandages scattered across his chest and stomach, covering the sutures. She had watched Henry stitch the wounds, lifting the maroon thread and snipping the ends, closing the skin like shells.

"I dreamed of sand," Benson said. "Everywhere. And everyone was sinking into it except me. I walked right over it. Right to the end." He kept his hands raised, swinging them lazily in the air.

She dipped a sponge into the water and worked around Junpei's bandages, scrubbing his body. The soap smelled of dust. She hummed to herself, tracing the shape of his shoulders.

She spoke of her day, the blind boy she had recently met. She told him he would have liked the marbles.

"I saw a house once," Benson continued while she washed Junpei's neck. "It had collapsed sideways like a tree. The whole structure. It lay in the middle of an unpaved street. You see. Like this." Benson tilted his arms over the bed.

Miya pressed the sponge against Junpei's cheeks, the water running down onto the pillow. She told him of the shirt she had made. For when he woke. She watched Junpei's mouth as Benson's voice came to her, hovering by the curtain.

"An older couple lived there," he said. "They had arranged the furniture to accommodate their new floor, which had once been their wall. They refused to leave. The husband was shaking a grenade. His wife stood by the sideways window. She had silver hair. She wore a brooch on her shirt, a flower, a star, I don't remember. I asked to take the wife. The husband refused. I motioned for her to leave. 'Come out the window,' I said. It was open, no glass. She reached through it and took my hand. She squeezed my fingers. Her palms were warm. I could smell her insides. And that's the last thing I remember."

Water droplets ran across Junpei's chest, carrying the light of stars. It was the nose, she thought, that remained from his boyhood. The flat bridge. His lips, too. The sharp angle of his jaw. She knew them well.

"You moved the stones," she said, rubbing the gauze

wrapped over Junpei's forehead. "After the painter finished. You formed the shape of an arrow."

She took Junpei's fingers and placed them between her teeth. She trimmed his nails, which tasted of flour, and swallowed each crescent sliver.

"There," she said. "All better."

A light flashed across the ward then faded. The sound of a car passing the main road. The soft clatter of a nurse's footsteps approaching a coughing patient.

"Some nights I dream that house is still there," Benson went on. "It's grown roots. It's sunk. A window is used as a door. The couple's still there, way down below, waving." He turned his head in her direction for the first time. "Doll face," he said. "When you sleep next to that man. I don't know why you do. But you talk in your sleep."

She looked across at Benson. She waited for him to go on. The night had thinned and the floor of the ward shone. Benson returned to staring at the ceiling. He stretched his hands into moonlight, as if attempting to take hold of it, and then brought them down over his eyes. His lips moved but what he said she didn't hear. Her vision blurred. She wiped her face and looked down at the body she had just washed. "I never left," she said.

Someone touched her shoulder. It was suddenly morning, the light of day abundant. Her eyes focused on Henry standing beside her. And then she saw a woman at the foot of the bed. She had a receding hairline and long fingers. She wore a shirt that wrapped across her chest and a long skirt that billowed. She was running her hands over Junpei's toes. Miya smiled, thinking this a dream. "You're here," she said, taking Junpei's hand.

Henry was watching her but she thought little of it. The woman was crying, staring at the body on the bed.

"It's all right," Miya said. "I've kept your sewing machine."

"Miya," Henry said, and took her shoulder again. He leaned forward and spoke into her ear. "Miya. Are you listening?"

She nodded. "It's in my room. Little Betty, it's called."

"Miya. Listen to me."

His voice was steady. She looked to see if Benson was awake but he wasn't.

"Do I talk in my sleep?" she asked Henry, and he didn't answer. He pointed at Junpei. The blanket was pulled up to his waist and folded back. His shirt lay open and she apologized, reaching to button it.

Henry took her wrist. He spoke as if from a distance, though she could feel his breath against her cheeks, soft as wings. "The woman here. This is the boy's mother. She heard about her son and has come to visit him. Do you understand, Miya?"

"Which boy?"

Henry pointed at Junpei. "This one."

"He doesn't have a mother," Miya said. She smiled at him with patience. "Neither of us does. I told you, Henry. Ages ago. Remember?"

"It's time to stop," Henry said. "It's my fault. I'm sorry, Miya. His mother's here now. She'll be staying with him. You can help the others. Like we agreed." He gripped her arms. "Let's go," he said. "You need to rest."

Miya refused to move from the chair, placing her hands underneath her legs. She turned to the woman. "I kept it. Like you said. I make clothes now." She struggled against Henry's hands, twisting her shoulders. He called her name, a bit louder now, though the more he did so his voice seemed to fade and she stood quickly and leaned over Junpei and held his face. Then she tore away the gauze and lifted his eyelids and saw the emptiness there, a pair of tunnels. The mother began to shout. There were footsteps. She was embraced.

"Junpei," she whispered into where his eyes should have been. "Junpei. I have yet to find it."

She was pulled as if tied to a string and she fell backward, her legs giving way. She was caught and dragged across the ward. Her gown skimmed the floor. She watched Henry's body diminish, bending down to pick up her nurse's cap. She saw Junpei's feet, the woman still touching them. The faces of the convalescents passed by her, tall as trees. Out the window the hills swallowed clouds.

.   .   .

Later in the day, Henry visited her room. She had been using the sewing machine and he sat at the edge of the desk and placed his clipboard beside her. A small bandage covered her arm, her skin sore from an injection they had given her. She continued to sew, feeding the fabric through the machine. He looked down at her fingers. "Careful," he said, and smiled.

"You have lists," Miya said. "Like Miss Hara."

"That's right," he said. He showed her a piece of paper with her name at the top and a paragraph in his handwriting that he would not let her read. There were dates along the margins as well. *1951* was the first.

"You haven't been taking your medicine," he said.

"I don't have headaches," she said, cranking the wheel.

"Sometimes you have them without realizing, Miya. That's why you should take the medicine. It's for your health that I give them to you. I wouldn't do it if I thought otherwise. Over two years it's been. Since you came. Since we've known each other."

She finished a torn shirt and moved on to a pair of pants.

"You're a great help to us," he said. "You help the wounded. You always have. And always will. I am indebted. But it's getting worse, you see. I think you know that. Each time. Promise me you'll take them."

She listened to footsteps in the corridor. Henry rubbed his face and she saw his tiredness again.

"There should be paintings," she said. "In the hallways."

"There aren't any," he said. "I've told you this. And there isn't a blind child either. Now promise to take your medicine."

She hesitated, then agreed.

"Good," he said, and handed her a small tin cup. He watched her take them, swallow, and then he leaned down and carelessly sifted through her fabrics. "We wouldn't like it either," he said. "To be thought of as someone else."

He settled the nurse's cap on her head and tucked a loose strand of her hair behind her ears. He stood to go but paused at the door and watched her. She pretended not to notice. When the American couple had brought her here, she clutched the sewing machine against her stomach, unwilling to part with it. "A volunteer," Henry had said. "Help is always needed." Together they watched the couple leave by car down the road. "It isn't far," Henry said, and patted her shoulder. "Just across the hills."

One night after the woman came for her son, Miya saw the blind boy. She was in her room, unable to sleep, and heard a strange sound coming from outside the window, not unlike something being dragged across the dirt. She rose and placed her elbows onto the ledge and scanned the lawn, the footpaths, and the gate.

The boy was directly below her. He sat on a bicycle. Its frame seemed to engulf him. The handles were wide and his arms were outstretched, clinging to the bars. He circled the courtyard, the wheels creating a circle in the dirt, which he followed without error.

"There you are," she said quietly against the windowpane.

She undressed and slipped into the clothes she had worn when she first arrived here, a pair of old pants and a shirt Miss Hara had given her on a birthday. It was imprinted with flowers and she had said it came from England. Miya took out her satchel from under the bed and placed her comb and Miss Hara's teacup into it. She couldn't find her shoes, so she left barefoot and tiptoed down the corridor and down the stairs. At the ward she paused by the door and heard Benson muttering. Through a space in the curtain she saw the comatose patient lying with a blanket tucked under his chin. The man's mother was sitting on a chair beside him. Her posture was straight and she held a book out in front of her, reading under a lamp.

Miya left them and walked down the hallway to the main entrance. She pushed the door open and stepped outside, her body caught by a breeze. The entire courtyard was lit by a heavy moon above the hills. The snow on the far ridges had begun to melt. It was quiet, save for the gears of the bicycle. She approached the boy, who stopped pedaling and placed his feet on the ground. Tonight, he was wearing a cotton engineer's cap that drooped past his ears.

"Hey, Miss," he said. "Want to ride?"

He waved his arm behind him. She raised a leg and sat on

the seat. He took his cap off and placed it on her head. "Hold on to my waist," he said. He was thin and she felt his hipbones push up against her palms. Like before, he carried a pouch tied to his belt loop. She lifted her feet. He stood and began to pedal and the bicycle swayed from their weight. She clung to him. "Miss," he said. "Not so tight." She relaxed. Soon, they were moving down the driveway.

"I pedal," the boy said. "You tell me where we're going."

They reached the end of the hospital property and passed under the gates. "Left," she said, and the boy swerved and she held him and began to laugh. "Stop!" she called. "Stop."

"You're not very good at this," the boy said, braking.

She got off the bicycle and walked to the fences. She twisted her hair up and hid it underneath the cap, lowering the brim to just above her eyes. A few of the windows of the main hall were lit and she could distinguish the silhouettes of the nurses walking through the wards. She used to take Junpei here, in those days after they had posed for the painter. She would help him climb the fence, holding his waist. They would shout, "Give us back our faces!" And if anyone approached them, they would run away.

The blind boy tugged on her sleeve. "We go on?"

"We go on."

They continued down the road, following the fences and the hills. The hospital began to shrink from view. Stars gathered along the crests of the distant mountains. They could smell the sea. He pedaled faster. Their bodies pulsed in the darkness. She wondered, as she did sometimes, whether her parents were still underground. A city rebuilt on top of them. It seemed possible.

"Hey, Miss," the boy said. "War's ending." He tapped his earlobe. "Listen."

THE HANGING LANTERNS
OF IDO

AT DUSK THE IRON LANTERNS on the arches above the boardwalk began to light, one by one, starting at the wharf and trailing west along the northern coast of the island. Dim at first, they soon pulsed, like a multitude of hearts, until at last their glow turned continuous. They had been installed months ago, in the spring, the first of the many renovations planned for the port city in the new millennium. And like all the days since, from one season to the next, the visitors came steadily throughout the evening. They moved slowly down the wide path, in pockets, browsing the stalls where the merchants sold an assortment of goods, including tapestries, jewelry, and kites. Lines were formed for hot tea and noodle soups. Children, having had their share of fried dough, gathered on the shore, counting ships. The sun receded, and from the point of a promontory a lighthouse illuminated the sea.

It was October. A Saturday. This was the neighborhood

of Ido in Solla City. And among the pedestrians at this hour was a young couple who had been married for several years. Their names were Isun and Taeho. They were dressed in the popular styles of that autumn, the woman wearing a long pale coat, her husband in a brown two-button suit. From afar, you would not have noticed them among the crowd. In their appearance they were no different from the other modern couples who had, in the past ten years, gained from the island's flourishing economy and who were now enjoying the evening on the boardwalk. Isun was a manager at the Lotte Hotel, which loomed above the coast. Taeho was a bookkeeper for the island's tourism bureau.

Every so often they paused beside the stalls, where miniature domes of steam hovered over the vendors as they cooked and placed their food on warm plates for display. A man wearing plastic gloves cupped a dumpling shell in his palm and scooped two fingers full of ground pork and vegetables into the shell's middle. He then lined the edges of the shell with egg yolk and closed the dumpling, pinching the ends together. He repeated the process, creating a dozen with speed and confidence, and then dropped them into a pot of boiling water.

"Do you wish I could do that?" Isun leaned toward Taeho's ear. She asked this whenever they came here, referring to her limits in the kitchen. "Admit it," she said. "A part of you wishes I could."

"Every evening," he said, and she poked his stomach with her finger.

"You're awful," she said. "An awful, awful man."

They continued their walk heading west, unhurried, Taeho with his hands clasped behind his back. Isun slipped an arm around his. The sky had finished its transition, revealing stars. The night colors arrived: office lights and streetlamps, the fluorescence of blinking storefront signs. There was a wind but they did not mind it. The walk was a habit they had formed during the weekends, a routine that marked their times of leisure. They were now deciding on where to have dinner, whether to stop at a stall or return to the boulevard in the city center. Passing under the lanterns their faces brightened then shadowed and brightened again. It was, so far, an ordinary Saturday.

In the end they decided on a Thai restaurant not far from their apartment, one they dined at often since their marriage. They were now familiar with the place. The corner booth, in their fantasies, theirs. Out of formality they opened their menus even though they already knew what they wanted. When a waitress approached them they pretended to consider the daily specials, printed on an extra sheet of paper.

And it was only when they heard a voice, "Could I get you something to drink?" that they raised their heads, and Isun said, "Iced tea, please," and Taeho realized, as his wife spoke, that the girl was new. Their eyes met and he smiled and she hesitated. "The same," he said. "Please." The girl did not reply. She stood there looking at Taeho and he continued to smile, amused, admitting that she was pretty with her small nose and dark eyes, her hair tied back and falling past her narrow shoulders. He repeated himself in case she had not heard and was waiting for him to order a drink. He spoke a third time and then a sadness fell over the girl's face, the way her lips pressed together and her eyes seemed to bare themselves and dampen.

"I'm sorry," Taeho said. "Is everything all right?" He glanced at Isun, who had returned to reading the menu and only now brought her attention upon the situation.

The girl continued to stare at him. After a moment, she said, "It's you."

"It's you," she repeated, and lifted her hand to cover her mouth as if she had spoken when she shouldn't have or that she herself was surprised at what came forth, this loosening of her tongue, the unexpected forming of words, released, and within them a recognition.

In some ways it was a simple case of mistaken identity. Taeho resembled a man whom she once knew. Just like him, the girl said. But he was dead. He had been on a motorbike. A delivery truck was ill-prepared for the coastal roads. This was in Phuket, in Thailand. Two years ago.

As Taeho listened, his chest went hollow. She spoke all this in haste, as if it were an afterthought. Then she stopped and said nothing further about the man. Instead she wrote their orders down on a small pad of paper and left. "Poor girl," Isun said, when they were alone. "She thought you were a ghost." She took his hand in hers and squeezed. She shook her head, saying, "That's terrible. What an awful thing," and he said, "Yes. Awful," and they were silent.

Above them hung a framed photograph of an aerial view of the Phuket coast. Taeho studied it for some time, the translucent water that was emerald in some portions, the color of the sky in others. The sand was pale, the land curved and speckled by tiny shapes that he guessed were sunbathers. They had thought of spending their honeymoon in Phuket, when it seemed everyone was going there. But they had changed their minds and remained in Solla, driving to the southern coast, visiting the waterfalls, the caves, and the hill town where they browsed the crafts stores and toured the watchtower at its crest. It seemed so long ago, right then, staring at the photograph on the wall. He could no longer recall why they had decided against it.

"I hope we haven't put her in an awkward position," Isun said. "I'd hate that. Do you think she'll work the other tables instead?"

"I think she'll be fine," he said.

"Yes, I suppose so. And then we'll leave and by tomorrow she'll forget it ever happened."

"Maybe it happens often," he said, wondering if the man

the waitress once knew haunted her like this, in the guise of others.

"Like a recurring dream," Isun said. "A bad one. Look. There she is."

They both averted their gazes, Isun glancing at two businessmen sitting by the bar, their shoulders hunched, tall Japanese bottles of beer beside them. Taeho returned his attention to the photograph.

The Thai girl approached them, carrying their dinner on a large tray. She had washed her face and her skin shone and was blushed around her eyes and Taeho imagined her excusing herself to the boss and entering the rear restroom for the employees. He thought this but was surprised to find that he did not pity her. It wasn't that. So what was it then? He stiffened his back as she smiled professionally. She told them to be careful because the plates were hot, and he held his breath until she returned to the front of the restaurant where she spent a few minutes joking with another waitress. He watched her. Isun began to eat. She mentioned the food was what they had ordered. The girl hadn't made a mistake.

And throughout their dinner the waitress was, as Taeho had said, fine. As if it had never happened. She came often to the table to see how they were. She was courteous. When they finished she bowed and said, "Come again," in a cheerful manner and walked them to the door, waving.

They walked home down the boulevard, under the trees,

the city dark and lit by shop windows and traffic. From a car radio came an American song Taeho recognized but could not quite place: a man's voice, a slow guitar. They passed a woman leaning out of a third floor window, laughing, the ash from her cigarette glowing for an instant like a firework. In the park a boy sat alone on a bench, sharing his hamburger with his dog. Taeho kept his hands in his pockets and rubbed his thumb against the teeth of his apartment key. Isun rested her head on his shoulder. She told him they were lucky. He wrapped an arm around her. And then it appeared as though she, too, forgot about the incident. She did not speak of it again.

They lived on the twelfth floor of a high-rise and later, as they prepared for bed, she used the bathroom first and he listened to her brush her teeth. "Don't brush so hard," he said, when she came out. She rolled her eyes at him. He ignored the gesture. He shut the bathroom door and looked at himself in the mirror. He traced the outline of his jaw with his fingers.

It had happened a few times, people thinking he was someone else, a person tapping him on the shoulder. It happened to everyone, he assumed. It was, usually, a cause for a brief moment of embarrassment. But afterward he didn't think anymore about the incident and he was quite sure the person who had approached him didn't think anymore about it either. But this was different, although he wasn't sure how or why. Perhaps because the man whom he resembled was dead. Or perhaps it wasn't that at all. Perhaps it was the girl herself. The phrase, "It's you," and the expression of her face that spoke of the possibility that perhaps she had been wrong, that he had been alive all this time. He felt those words and her conviction, which had lasted only for an instant but nonetheless remained with him like an extra layer of skin.

When he joined Isun in bed she shut off the bedside lamp. She fell asleep quickly. He smelled the mint of her breath. He shut his eyes. He thought perhaps that all that luck meant was that you weighed your own life against someone else's and yours turned out to be better. And where was the good in that? And what would his wife have done? If he was the one who was now gone? Would she find a man who resembled him? And what would happen then?

He watched the minutes pass on his bedside clock. He had a sudden urge to talk to Isun but chose not to wake her. He wanted to tell her, as if she hadn't heard, that he resembled a man a world away and two years dead. He wanted to tell her that he had never ridden a motorbike. Not even a scooter or a moped, though there were so many on the island. He wanted to ask her whether his life would be different if he had done so. He tried to picture this man; it should have been easy—it was his face, after all—but the harder he concentrated the more he felt it slipping. As a child, he would try to grip the mist that clouded the harbor. He thought you could. He moved his hand into it and made a fist and what lay in his palm felt like feathers.

. . .

At the tourism bureau the following week all the employees were discussing the provincial government. In the coming month, it was reported, they would announce a proposal for turning the island into a visa-free territory. This would allow foreign investors unrestricted access to build their own tourist venues, such as casinos and hotels, and even to establish schools. It had been a plan that had, at first, seemed bold and ambitious to Taeho. But now he was no longer sure of its intentions and the more his colleagues discussed the profit of such a venture the less interested he became in its details.

It was still early in the morning. He had retreated into his office. He pressed the back of his hand against the window to feel the cold from this height and saw that the day would be beautiful. On the horizon a cruise liner, the color of a stone, was making its way through the strait and out toward the great body of the Pacific. He wondered who it held. From where they embarked. Where they were going.

In the office next to his was the bureau's library, filled with guidebooks on various countries. They kept track of the reviews and recommendations, the development of trends, the hotels that offered free yoga classes, entire sections devoted to sushi restaurants. A fluorescent light hung from the ceiling giving the space a bright glow that appeared independent of time; in there it could have been morning or evening, it did not matter.

He found the books for Thailand. He chose the thickest one, its spine unblemished, although it was older, dust along its edges, the pages faded. A telephone rang somewhere on the floor. He heard the wheels of the mail crate rumble past his office. He flipped through the book until he came to a set of photographs of Phuket. The first was of the town, its gray buildings much like Solla. The other was of a coastal hotel, tall and wide, with rectangular windows, each with its own balcony. He was about to turn the page but stopped. At a corner window, up toward the right, there was a figure. Or part of one, the rest behind a curtain. He saw a bare leg, an arm, he was sure of it. He looked closer. Half a face. Man or woman, he couldn't tell. The hair blended against the dark of the hotel room, the body—or what he could distinguish of it—too distant. Perhaps the person had seen the camera. Perhaps it was a holiday, a tryst, a honeymoon. Perhaps the person was alone.

He thought of how sometimes on the weekends Isun left for a meeting at the hotel. He would go to her and say, "Goodbye, see you soon," and she would say, "See you," and then he would shut the door and cross the room and press his forehead against the windowpane. There he waited. And although spotting her from so high was, he knew, impossible, he attempted to always. He imagined the route she took, crossing the street and heading several blocks west and then another block south. He imagined her raising her arm to push the revolving door of the hotel entrance and then crossing the marble-floored hallway, greeting the receptionists, and taking another elevator up to the twentieth floor where she walked into a conference room with a wall of windows facing him. And then, picturing this, Taeho waved.

Their years had been constant and steady. He used to think they always would be.

In their early days they were shy. They undressed in the dark. He would close his eyes in that dark and press his palms against her chest, her hand guiding his. He wanted to concentrate on her skin, to know how she felt before he saw her; he would touch her and imagine what she looked like. The first time he saw her in the light, she stood framed within their bedroom door. She had flicked the switch on impulse. He covered himself then flung the sheet away. She said to him, "Well, now you know all there is to know." She placed a hand on her hip and her finger pointed to a mole on the ride side of her waist as if that were her secret. He had never noticed it before.

He remembered a sense of sadness coming to him then. Not because of her or her body but the fact that his hands hadn't discovered this raised dark circle, this small coin. He had not touched her completely. He had tried. Yet there were still places he missed. She approached him and lay down on top of the red duvet and took his hand. She kissed him and the sadness lifted and he loved her and she said, "Here," and, "There," and her skin was warm and trembling.

. . .

In the afternoon they met on the boardwalk. She couldn't stay long, she told him. From a sea woman she chose a platter of abalone. Taeho, from the neighboring stall, ordered Udon noodles, served in a large ceramic bowl. Many of the benches were already occupied by tourists and the businessmen who worked nearby. Some even stood by the stalls, eating and talking to one another. The day was clear and bright and the winds were calm. At the wharf, men were loading and unloading cargo from the ships. Two men in suits left a bench and Taeho, balancing the noodle bowl in his hands, hurried to take it.

They sat facing the city, the ocean behind them. Behind the brick row houses, scattered among the three-story buildings, stood the towering panels of the Lotte Hotel, their apartment complex, and a few others not yet finished, the bright cranes beside them lifting steel. It was said in Solla you could judge a building's age by its height. The modern ones were no shorter than ten stories. Spaces were bought; buildings were demolished, new ones were built. It was a city at once shrinking and growing. It was most evident during the day, when the colors of the architecture defined themselves against the blue sky. At night, the colors were of lights, a great ocean of them, and where one building ended and another began was not as distinct.

Isun, between bites of her abalone, pointed her chin at a man sitting a few benches away, facing the sea. "He's new,"

she said. "Started a few days ago. I feel old when I see him."
The man wore a pin-striped suit and a gold-colored tie. With
his jacket unbuttoned he hunched forward, eating a sandwich.
He was handsome, Taeho admitted, and wondered if that was
what Isun had meant. A group of women passed the man and
he glanced up at them. "Shall we have him over for dinner
sometime?" she asked. "He just moved here. From Seoul. I
think he's lost." She smiled, brushing her hands together and
standing. She always felt obliged to host a dinner for the new
employees. They did so often.

"All right," Taeho said, looking up at her. He handed her
his empty bowl, the chopsticks placed inside. "Return this,
too?"

She carried their dishes to the vendors, handing hers over
to the sea woman and then the bowl to the noodle maker. The
young man, who, upon seeing her, quickly stood, bits of his
sandwich falling from his shirt as he wiped his mouth with
the back of his hand and bowed. Isun, whenever she laughed,
brought her hands together as though in prayer and Taeho
watched her do this now, thinking that standing beside the man
she did in fact seem older. Perhaps it was the way she stood
there, her posture not as straight as it once was. She had also
gained weight in the hips. He watched her lips move. She was
too far away for him to be able to discern what she was saying,
although it was easy to guess. She was formal and courteous.
She pointed at Taeho and the man nodded with eagerness.

It was a good match, both their parents had said, during their courtship. They—the parents—had been referring to their children's careers and a sense of stability that they themselves had struggled for during the war and the years after. Throughout the ceremony, he caught their looks of approval and relief and felt the pride of a son and began to see a life unfolding in the way he had promised them. He imagined a future when he would be someone others looked toward and envied.

She went on talking, or the young man did, but Taeho's attention was diverted to the stalls where the sea woman raised her voice at the noodle maker. He couldn't hear exactly their words, something about the trawlers and their nets, and the noodle maker laughed and responded and she frowned and fell silent. She draped a towel around her hand and placed a fresh oyster on it. She picked up a small knife and inserted it near the hinge of the shell. She worked quickly until she had opened a dozen. The noodle maker, as if unsure whether he had won the argument, lost interest in the woman and dropped wheat noodles into a pot of boiling water.

"Hello." He heard Isun's voice and looked around to see her standing in front him. The young man stood beside her, bowing. Taeho asked if Isun had heard the argument. She introduced her coworker. "We'll have dinner next week," she said. A family passed behind them and took photographs of the shoreline and the ocean. "And no. I didn't hear an argument. We were speaking of airplanes. He likes to fly."

"I couldn't hear it either," Taeho said. "I wonder what it was about."

"Taeho." She leaned down and pressed her hand against his. "I wasn't paying attention."

The man bowed again and told them both he was looking forward to their evening. He then excused himself and returned to his bench. Isun, watching him, tapped a finger against her watch. She took Taeho's arm and, with a slight persistence, led him down the boardwalk. They passed the stalls and Taeho glanced back again at the sea woman selling the oysters she had shucked to a mother and her daughter. The lines on her face were as deep as chasms. Her eyes met his and, surprising him, she grinned as if they were old friends, and he looked away.

Crossing the street, he matched the rhythm of his wife's steps. The sun reflected off glass windows. Isun raised a hand over her eyes. "You said nothing to him," she said. "Not a thing." And then she left, heading to the hotel. Taeho returned to the offices. The rest of the day passed without event, without effort.

That evening, on his way home, he visited the Thai restaurant. The sun was setting, the sky bold and cloudless. On the street two teenagers honked the horns of their mopeds and raced through traffic. He paused by the restaurant windows and looked inside at the warm lights hanging from the ceiling, at the bar where a few customers had gathered. In the back of the dining area a waitress placed two plates on a table. He was too far away to see if it was her.

He kept recalling the event. He did not know why. It both frustrated him and pleased him. He thought of her flat lips, her thin arms pale as sun-bleached stones. And the more he did so, the more her words to him seemed like a hint, some kind of suggestion, as if she had briefly shown him a room that overwhelmed him with familiarity, a certainty that he had once spent time there.

He should have said something else. Or something more. He kept thinking of that as well. When the girl said, "You look just like him," he could have asked her if she had been referring to a specific part of him.

He and Isun used to describe each other. A game they played. It would begin with the question of how their faces differed from one another's, from everyone's. Taeho's eyes were in the shape of small shells. Isun's lips were arched slightly, like the curve of wings. Her cheekbones, like blades. Like protection.

"Tell me more," he could have said to the waitress as well, and she would recall a life and he would listen. She would tell him what sort of life that was. What sort of work the man did. The clothes he wore. Whether he was kind or stubborn or inconsiderate or violent. "And how did you come here?" he could ask her. He imagined their conversation as though it had already occurred, as though it were his memory.

But he had said nothing to the girl. Instead, he avoided her, focusing his attention on the white tablecloth and the weaves there. He rubbed his fingertips against the cloth and thought of mountain ranges and canyons and islands. And his heart, percussive, sped, as though across a body of water.

It did so again as he entered the restaurant. The city noises faded, taken over by music from the speakers above the bar and the clanking of glasses. The hostess, short with her long hair tied up into a bun and held together by a chopstick, greeted him. "Only you tonight?" she said.

"There was a waitress here," he said, describing her—her height, the cut of her hair, her eyes. "Last week. She served us dinner. Young."

"Yes?"

"Is she in tonight?"

The hostess frowned. She took him aside, to the wall where the diners hung their coats. "Is there a problem? Are you missing something?"

Taeho looked past her, at the waitresses he could see. "Problem? No. No, I'm not missing anything. I wanted to speak to her. She served our table last week, yes? You remember? She said I looked like someone she once knew. She was upset. Do you remember?" The hostess shook her head. "I was sorry," he went on. "I wanted to tell her that, you see. I never did. I wanted to tell her that I am sorry."

"Sir, she isn't here."

"When will she be in?"

The door opened and a couple entered. The hostess bowed to them, went to retrieve a pair of menus, and ushered them to a window seat. She returned and spoke quietly. She told Taeho that the girl no longer worked at the restaurant, that they had let her go.

"Let her go?"

The girl had taken money from the register. The bartender witnessed it. They found a roll of bills folded inside the waistband of her pants. They checked the register. It was missing money. She left and they never saw her again.

Taeho did not respond. He stood there and it was as though he were still hearing the hostess speak. She apologized to him, bowing.

"And the police?" he asked.

She looked about the room for a moment before meeting his eyes. "No trouble here," she said. "No trouble. Nothing, in the end, was stolen."

A family appeared. The hostess led them to the booth where he sat with Isun a few days before. A waitress took their orders. Her hair was braided and she laughed at something the father said.

Taeho returned outside. The air was cold. Linden trees swayed beside the streetlamps. He felt the lights of cars brush his arms and his legs. The shops were busy, their windows filled with mannequins in various positions, showcasing the latest fashions. At the corner of the street a crowd had gathered to watch a magician dressed in a tuxedo and wearing white gloves shuffle overturned cups on a table. The man was humming and when a girl pointed at a cup he lifted it with flourish and the crowd cheered.

He had been wrong. He pitied her. Yes, he thought. It had been a fancy.

He checked his watch. He hurried. Perhaps Isun was home already. He would cook for her tonight. It would be his apology for this afternoon. She would accept it, as she always did.

In recollection Taeho could say that he had felt an unease which he could not articulate and he had walked away. What that unease was he never identified. But it no longer seemed to matter. For Taeho, the restaurant and the woman now lasted in his mind for a single instant, compressed, as though he had taken her photograph and nothing else. He thought how insignificant it was in duration compared to the rest of his life and his years with Isun.

They took their routine walks. The weather grew colder but they grew accustomed to it. They invited guests to their apartment and hosted dinner parties for their coworkers. They went to the movies and the restaurants. They attended gallery openings and university lectures. They read aloud to each other newspaper articles about the shift to a visa-free international city, a lost fishing boat, territorial disputes with the

Japanese, and updates from the mainland. In this way every morning, beside the window of their apartment with its view of the city, they felt aware of this island and its place in the Pacific and even farther, toward the continent of Europe and the coasts of America.

On some days, however, it was as if they spoke of these things out of a forced will. To say something. There was a pretense there, a lack of comfort, as if they knew not what they spoke of, their words drifting. But this observation never grew into a concern and he dismissed it quickly.

All was as it had always been.

The months passed into winter. Taeho celebrated a birthday, his thirty-fifth. They took a week-long holiday and went to the southern coast, to a hotel that faced the East China Sea. It was where they had gone on their honeymoon and they had not returned since. They spent their days being tourists, as they had done before. They went to the caves and hiked the trails. They visited waterfalls. It was a reminder of who they were and who they had become and what they had earned and gained and all the time in between.

He was happy, he said to himself many times during their trip. He said it to her as well and took her hand but what he felt surprised him. It was the feeling of dreams, the ones he used to have before they married. He would find himself someplace, anyplace, his childhood home, a department store, the beach, and he would have a sudden desire to run. But he never could. As though something were pushing against him. "I can never run in dreams," he once told her, and she looked at him with patience.

One afternoon they went to the old watchtower at the crest of the hill town. The day was cold but the clouds parted on occasion, revealing the sun that reflected off the tiled rooftops of the houses along the slope. He recalled the tower's history from their first visit, the failed revolt against the Japanese sentinels during the occupation, and later, the Allied bombings that nearly destroyed the outpost. It was a museum now and had been renovated years ago to resemble how it once was. The walls were made of pale stones and on the peak of the wooden roof stood a copper weathervane. A small lamp hung in the gallery. Seabirds perched on the railings, clustered around a pair of binoculars that Taeho did not remember from before.

Some distance away from the tower, across the ridge, lay the barracks. It was made of the same type of stones, half of which was a replica of where the watchmen lived, the other half having been converted into a gift shop. Inside, a young woman sat behind a counter with a hand under her chin, reading. On occasion she spun a rack of postcards beside her.

When Isun began to walk into the shop, Taeho told her his stomach was bothering him. He would wait, he said, and she shrugged and after purchasing a ticket from the woman she crossed the hillcrest and entered the tower, the birds swiftly departing.

Taeho approached the barracks and looked through a window. It was a single long room, divided by rope, and on the other side of the shop he could see tatami mats, pads of paper, tin cups, a spyglass, and a bucket. On the far wall there was a gray uniform on a hook. Below that a pair of boots and a rifle. He moved to another window and his shadow fell on the young woman who suddenly stood up, startled, placing a hand on her chest. Then she laughed. She had long straight hair and wore a dress that was slightly too large for her. Her bracelets had slipped to her elbows. Taeho raised a hand in apology and stepped back.

The town descended gradually to the coast. The wind moved with a heaviness and he flipped up the collar of his coat. He watched his breath leave him. Clouds coursed overhead and he imagined the men who once lived here in these confines and he saw that they were boys and he saw them rise from their beds and carry the paraffin every evening at sundown, a long line of them walking the ridgeline. He saw them ascend the tower, their spyglasses swiveling over a sea that resembled a wide field of ash, waiting for ships.

Minutes later he spotted Isun above, circling the gallery, her body as small as a star. She waved and he returned it. The sun reflected off her fingers, a small point, and he saw her slip a coin into the binoculars. Leaning forward, her hair caught in the wind like some old flag, she swiveled the lens over the hill town, at all the stores they had browsed through when they had been married for less than forty-eight hours, at the same body of water they walked beside every day, and it all seemed to him then so purposeless.

How long she was up there he didn't know. It seemed to last for hours and yet when she returned it seemed she had just left. She asked whether he was feeling better and he said, "Yes, better," and they drove back through the town. She questioned how far the lamp of the tower could be seen in those days. "Not far," he said.

"Even so, it is beautiful," she said, and he responded, "Yes, we saw it before," and she tilted her head, studying him. "We did," she said. "Just as beautiful as then. That's what I meant."

That evening, he and Isun fought. They had decided to remain in the hotel room rather than go to a restaurant. They would rest, eat in. On the dresser was a celadon vase Isun had bought that afternoon from a potter in the town. It was slim, with a long neck, and incised with images of egrets in flight. "To match the other one," she said, reminding him of their first purchase together those years ago when they first came here. He smiled in response. She turned on the television and they lay in bed watching a show about movie stars. But soon Taeho's attention drifted and he stood and approached the window. His image and Isun's on the bed was transposed onto the glass, which gave way to a view of the sea and the veranda below where the tourists were dining. And for the first time in many months he recalled the Thai waitress and what she had shared. He thought of the dead, of yearning. He thought of a photograph, the glimpse of a body beside a hotel window, of coastal roads and motorbikes, of watchmen along a high ridge, and the images came to him one after another with a sense of inevitability.

"You're fidgeting," Isun called.

"It isn't very interesting," he said.

"Neither are you," she said.

He looked at her, stunned. She was sitting with her back against the headboard. She brought a pillow to her chest and hugged it, facing the television. She had meant it as a joke, she said. She rolled her eyes. He stared at her face and saw the age there, the weathering, what time did and what it had left to do. And then he, as though from a great distance, watched his body approach her and he heard his voice say, "Look at me." He slammed his open palm against the mattress and he watched her jump and retreat to the wall, clutching the pillow. He cursed her. Cursed her and her body and her work and how dull she was and how it was all her fault and the more he spoke the more her face seemed to return to him, as if it had faded, and he recognized the woman he had known and then he fell silent.

He left her there and walked through a field that led to the woods and the coastal mountains, the hotel receding behind him. As he walked farther, he heard the constant push of water approaching land. He smelled the sea. The clouds were fluorescent. And when it was too cold he hurried back and watched the television in the lobby. A group of tourists from the mainland had gathered in front of the elevators, some of them tired, others drunk, stumbling, loud. Up above, the ceiling was painted to resemble the morning sky. He thought it unbearable. He did not know what had made him do such a thing. His chest closed, then, slowly, opened. He concentrated on his breathing.

He did not return until late, Isun already asleep. He lay beside her. She moved toward him, dreaming, and he held her and attempted to match his breathing with hers. In this way, he, too, slept.

They never spoke of it. They never would. He was forgiven when she took his arm the following day as they descended the elevator. She was forgiven when he helped her with her coat. They hired a guide who took them to Tamra Mountain. And upon their return at dusk they stood out on the veranda of the hotel. The winds were slow, colors fading. He looked at his wife. Seven years ago they had married. And through it he had chosen a life. Or one came to him. And there were others he had left and were now too far in the distance for him to see anymore. He could no longer remember what they were. But he was sure they had existed. Convinced of it.

They leaned against the stone wall, looking down at a golf course and the faraway mountains. Isun shivered and he asked whether they should return indoors. They could walk through the hotel and view the shops, he said, then head up to the room. He took her arm. "Come," he said, but she would not move. Her face was brilliant against the deep light of the setting sun and he saw the beauty there, its freshness, like a stranger's. There were many years ahead of them.

She spoke without looking at him. She said, "Do you think we ought to have gone to Phuket?"

It was their honeymoon she was referring to. And then her eyes welled and she held her gaze on the mountains and the sea, refusing to acknowledge the clear lines, like strips of glass, that fell down her cheeks.

"Isun," he said, and brought his hand to her face but she waved it away and laughed quickly, as if she had been reminded of something and only now remembered. "I must be tired," she said.

"You'll catch a cold." He wrapped his arm around her shoulder. How small her body was. How thin. And the beauty he saw a moment before was all of a sudden gone, replaced by a weariness. There was always what you expected, wasn't there? he thought. There was always that. Even when you knew it was no longer there, it never went away, this feeling. That was faith.

"I'm sorry, Taeho," she said. "It's nice to get away. We seem very far from the city, don't we? I am enjoying it. A little holiday. And I am sorry if I ruined it." She smiled at him and placed her arms across her stomach. "I'm really all right," she said. "I am now. Truly."

"I do love you," he told her, and believed it.

Indoors, they looked about the lobby, up at the painted sky and the looming chandeliers, dozens of them in a single row. "It's a much prettier hotel," she whispered to Taeho. "Much prettier than mine." Behind the reception desk, the faces of clocks showed what time it was across the globe. It was five in the evening on the island. An hour had passed since his birthday. He had not realized it. Another year had gone.

In the time that followed their visit to the southern coast, Taeho remained late in the offices, his desire to return home diminishing. He grew less concerned with his work as well. Instead, he read the newspaper or a book on the couch. He listened to the building empty, the cleaners come in to vacuum. He took off his shoes. Sometimes he stood by the window and looked out at the speckled city and the blinking airplanes, growing larger as they descended. Fishermen returned to the coast. Just a few minutes, he would tell himself, but when he looked at his watch again an hour had passed.

It grew colder. Even so he walked to the harbor and waited for the sun to set and the lanterns under the arches to glow. He watched pedestrians and looked at their faces and thought of a story for each of them. He pictured them as ghosts, translucent and silent. He thought of his parents who were no longer living but had, in life, formed their own happiness, over time, and how much he had wept in their passing not only out of grief—he understood now—but because they took with them everything that was not told and shared, knowledge that he would never learn or discover. He considered the possibility that there were many kinds of love and as you experienced one, you felt the absence of all the others. He thought of a city perpetually opening onto the sea.

And it was on one of these nights that he saw, among the crowd on the boardwalk, the Thai waitress. Several months had gone by since he looked for her. It had snowed the previous evening, the first of that season, and it covered the city and spread out along the beach where a group of children were building miniature snowmen, an army of them, scattered about the coast. She leaned against a wooden arch and was watching them. She wore a long heavy coat and a scarf. Her hair was covered by a striped wool hat. She held a cup of ice cream, her breath blooming white. He approached her and stood beside her, looking out at the wharf and the moored boats. "It's you," he said.

She looked up at him casually, as though she had seen him every day. She appeared tired. She held up the cup, licking the spoon. "Pistachio," she said. "My favorite."

He listened to her voice and realized it sounded nothing like what he remembered. It was less clean, less fluid.

"I looked for you," he said. "Months ago. I went back. They told me you had left." He did not mention the money, although it seemed she knew what he meant, the way she shifted her weight from one leg to another and avoided his eyes. The steam from a vendor's stall shrouded them for a moment before the wind took it away. "And you're well?" Taeho said, and did not know what more to say.

He tried to remember the questions he had for her. He wanted to know whether she had been in the accident, too. Or whether she had witnessed it. He wanted to know why she had, of all places, come here. Whether she had left or had run away. There were more. He tried to remember them all but was unable to. There seemed to be so many. And the more he attempted to recall them the less urgent they became. As though these weren't the questions he wanted to ask at all, as though the one language he knew had now failed him.

He followed the passage of a distant boat on the horizon. The vessel moved fast, like a satellite, and he imagined everyone he had ever known and had yet to meet aboard it, forever circling this earth.

"Phuket," he said. "I will go there." He looked at the girl. She was just a child.

"But everyone's coming here," she said, smiling briefly. Dusk was settling and the lanterns began to light, fogged by the snow. The girl pointed up at them. "Where I am from," she said, "we light a lantern for every missing sailor and hang it in front of our homes. For them to find us. And for them to know that we are waiting."

She stepped closer to him. Her skin was as pale as he

remembered. She raised her hand and touched his cheek. It lasted only for a moment. Her fingers were cold. She retreated and smiled again. "So strange," she said.

Did you love him? he wanted to say. Was there at least that?

And no matter how much he did not want her to leave, she did, backing away and then turning. He stepped forward to follow her but did not go any farther. He stood beside the wooden arch and watched as the girl moved through the crowd, past the pedestrians and the merchants, the sea woman and the noodle maker, still bickering. He could still distinguish her hat. On occasion she lifted a spoonful of ice cream to her lips. Then she was gone. A wind came and raised the settled snow once more. The flakes glowed against the lights and on the shore they fell again upon all the children carrying their snowmen into the water.

When Taeho opened the door to his apartment he found the rooms dark and the curtains open. The city shone silver onto the wooden floor. Out the window the stars were clear and vast. Leaving the lights off, he crossed the room and sat down on the couch. Beside him, on a small table, lay the guidebook he had taken from the library. He had brought it home months ago and had forgotten about it. Under the city lights he examined the pictures again. He could no longer distinguish the body at the window, as if he had dreamt it. He closed the book and listened to the muted sound of an airplane ascending.

Against a wall, on a shelf, stood a pair of slim celadon vases, the ones he and Isun had bought, seven years apart. In that dark he studied their form and design, their long necks. He remembered that there had been a potter in his family, a distant relative. The man lived on the mainland and Taeho's parents would, every year, receive a parcel from him. They let Taeho open the packages and he sifted through the straw to reveal a single dish or a bowl, trays and tea cups. Each one he dusted with a cloth and his father would carry him as he placed the gifts all throughout the house. And on nights when he could not sleep he spent the hours staring into the images depicted on their surfaces, the white willows, the curve of a river, a forest.

Taeho had not thought of the potter in many years. They had never met. One day, the parcels stopped coming. He was unaware if the man had children.

He heard the lock of the door twist. And then the room was flooded with the brightness of the hallway and the view from the window dimmed, replaced by a reflection of Isun's silhouette. She gasped, startled. "Taeho?" she said. He raised his arm at her reflection and waved slightly. She shut the door. Her heels clicked against the floor as she approached him. For a moment she remained standing with her fingers on the armrest of the couch, and then she sat beside him and crossed her legs. He smelled liquor on her breath. "New coat?" he said.

She fingered its lapels. The coat was tweed, the color red. She said yes, then paused. It was as though she wanted to say more but could not.

He turned to her. He said, "If you ever go away, I will remember your face."

"Taeho," she said.

"And I will look for it."

"Taeho, stop."

"Among a thousand faces. There will be yours. And mine. And we will look for each other. We will be strong. We will be heroic."

He said nothing more. They remained on the couch, facing the window, and listened to each other breathing. They were each waiting for the other to speak. In silence she reached for him and rested her head on his shoulder, and in this way they watched the passing of evening, the traffic on the roads, the faint shapes of bodies moving through rooms. Buildings faded. Everywhere there was snow. In the far distance the flash of a lighthouse swung across the sea and then stilled.

AUTHOR'S NOTE

"Once the Shore" was inspired by the tragedy involving
the Japanese fishing vessel, *Ehime Maru*; certain details of
this story were gathered from various sources pertaining to
Cheju/Jeju Island. "Among the Wreckage" is based on the
U.S. bombing that occurred in the vicinity of Dok Island
(Dokdo) in the summer of 1948. Some of the details in "So
That They Do Not Hear Us" were taken from a February
2005 *New York Times* article by Norimitsu Onishi. The
tale of the farmer and the maiden in "The Woodcarver's
Daughter" is loosely derived from the story "The Woodcutter
and the Heavenly Maiden" in *Korean Folk and Fairy Tales*, by
Suzanne Crowder Han (Hollym, 1991); the cave of offerings
is a variation on the village shrines depicted in *Myths of
Korea*, by Seo Dae-seok and Peter H. Lee (Jimoondang
Publishing Company, 2000). The last line of "The Hanging
Lanterns of Ido" was inspired by the last line of the story
"Island" by Alistair MacLeod in *Island: The Complete Stories*
(Norton, 2001). Also indispensable was: *Korea's Place in the
Sun: A Modern History* by Bruce Cumings (Norton, 1997).

*

Although I have used historical events and the descriptions
of actual islands in South Korea to form Solla Island, I have
altered history, geography, custom, and culture to suit the

purposes of these fictions. The name of the island and some
of the names of the characters are from my imagination.
As for the spelling of Korean names and places, I have
mostly used the McCune-Reischauer system and the revised
Romanization system; in some instances I disregarded both.

*

I share this book with all my friends and teachers and
colleagues throughout the years.

Thank you to the editors of the journals where these
fictions were first published; to Ralph Sneeden at Phillips
Exeter Academy and Anne Greene at Wesleyan University;
to the Ledig House Writer's Colony, where this book started,
and to Bill Clegg; to PEN/New England, Grub Street, and
the St. Botolph Club Foundation. To Yu Young-nan and Chi-
Young Kim. To Russell Perreault, Reed Maroc, Nayon Cho,
and Vintage Books; to Giulia Melucci and Harper's Magazine;
to Michael Collier, Jennifer Grotz, Noreen Cargill, and the
Bread Loaf Writers' Conference. To Percival Everett, Amy
Hempel, Andrew Sean Greer, Alexander Chee, and Eliza
Griswold. To Benjamin Percy, Bret Anthony Johnston, and
Josh Weil. To Kevin Doane, Nick Singer, and Adam Sadler.
To Susannah Geltman. To Melanie Rehak and Noah Isenberg.
To Calder Gillin and Jaime Gross. And to Alexandra Smith.

I am especially grateful to Ann Patchett, Katrina
Kenison, Andrea Barrett, Stacey Swann, Jill Meyers, Michael
Lowenthal, Scott Heim, and Robin Lippincott.

To Mitchell Waters at Curtis Brown, Ltd. To Sarah Gorham, Kirby Gann, Nickole Brown, and Jennifer Woods at Sarabande Books.

To Don Lee for his generosity. To Hannah Tinti for taking a chance.

To my great friend Ethan Rutherford.

And to Laura van den Berg, who was beside me from the first word to the last.

PY

THE AUTHOR

Paul Yoon was born in New York City. His fiction has appeared in *One Story, Ploughshares, TriQuarterly, Glimmer Train, American Short Fiction, The PEN/O. Henry Prize Stories* and *The Best American Short Stories,* among other publications. *Once the Shore* is his first book.

Peter Yoon